Sissy Holmes
and
The Case of the Dead
Hypnotist

By Mary Stojak

I hope you
enjoy and that's silly
see you next time!
Mary

Paperback ISBN 978-1-80424-071-7
ePub ISBN 978-1-80424-072-4
PDF ISBN 978-1-80424-073-1

Published by Orange Pip Books
335 Princess Park Manor, Royal Drive, London, N11 3G
www.orangepipbooks.com

Cover design by Brian Belanger

Chapter One

Only death would cure me. I'd tried everything to quit smoking—well, almost everything. My friend El wanted me to try hypnotism, but I had a bad feeling about letting anyone mess around inside my head.

"At least give it a try," she said after I told her I'd changed my mind.

El had been my best friend since my beloved husband Harry passed away. (Maybe beloved was too much? Loved, yes, I had loved him.) El and I had known each other before, but we became a lot closer after Harry's funeral. She had no trouble keeping me busy those first months when I was so lost. We visited the abundant number of museums in Washington, D.C. on the weekends and holidays.

"I know I told you I'd try anything," I replied. I didn't want to admit I was afraid. The pounding of a jackhammer down the side street in Bethesda made it impossible to say more.

El pulled me across the gray marble floor to the elevator inside the glass and steel building.

"Just a minute," I protested and slid a cigarette out of the pack in my purse. My other hand closed around the red plastic lighter in my pocket.

"It's nine-fifty-five and your appointment is at ten." El's caramel skin flushed. She grabbed the extra-long cigarette from my hand and threw it across the floor where it landed within an inch of a black lady's sturdy shoe. The woman flashed me a smile; it reminded me of my mother's smile when she brushed my hair. Both she and my father had died in a car crash when I was fourteen. I thought I'd been making my own decisions before the accident but found myself adrift without my mother's constant support and my father's firm rules.

If I hadn't been lost in the past, I might have picked up the cigarette and walked out the door. Instead, I followed El into the elevator.

Come to think of it, smoking a pipe like Sherlock Holmes might be cool. My bad habit was as much a part of me as the wrinkles that burst from the corners of my eyes.

But I really was determined to quit.

After Harry's funeral, I'd started smoking one or two cigarettes a day. Now, in the two years since he died, I smoked a pack-and-a-half a day. I must have forgotten how hard it would be to quit without him looking over my shoulder. And there was my lovely Dr. Venkatesan, my primary care physician, who also wanted me to quit. "With your luck," he'd said, "You'll get the Big C."

When the elevator doors slid open, the hallway looked like any other hallway. The hypnotist's office was like any other office. I have to admit I was disappointed. No red lights, no crystal balls, no humped-back servant telling me that lady so-and-so was communing with the spirits. The space didn't seem right, filled with comfortable beige chairs, a large mirror, and prints of small-town life. They weren't those old *Saturday Evening Post* prints I loved. Upon closer inspection, the people in the prints had rat faces even though the colorful pictures looked cheerful from a distance.

I snorted. When I showed El, she laughed behind her hand in such a refined way that I was immediately embarrassed by my reaction. She pointed at a black bug with orange spots coming out of a lady's mouth. "I wonder if that's her impression of people."

"I thought it was funny," a voice said behind us.

In the mirror to my left, I saw the reflection of a middle-aged woman with bleached-blond hair, slightly overweight, who probably shouldn't have been wearing a pink suit. Coming face-to-face with the hypnotist, I was surprised to see her pink glasses were embedded with a row of rhinestones—not what I expected from a professional.

"I'm Sissy Holmes." My maiden name rolled off my tongue like I'd been saying it all my life. For the last thirty-five years I'd used my husband's name Carpenter.

Dr. Randall smiled.

Changing my name hadn't bothered her at all. There was something else behind those pink glasses besides a slightly tacky lady. "That must be your maiden name," she said.

I nodded. "Is it okay for my friend to come in with me?"

Her smile disappeared. "Some people are very resistant to hypnosis. If they're distracted, they're impossible to put under."

The hypnotist's smile made another appearance. The change was so fast, I wasn't sure if I'd seen that childish pout. I didn't want to tell her I was afraid of what she might do to me, intentional or not.

"I understand," she said as if she'd read my thoughts. "Hypnotism is perfectly safe. And of course, your friend will probably be hypnotized, too." Dr. Randall gestured to a door bathed in pink light.

El frowned. "I'll wait for you here. We can leave the door open a crack."

Dr. Randall looked as if she wanted to scold us for wasting her time. "Absolutely not. I don't want to leave the door open to the waiting room. The next patient might disturb us."

"Come on," I said to El. After all, I didn't really believe Dr. Randall could hypnotize either one of us. Plus, the good doctor would charge me whether I took the treatment or not.

Inside the glowing room, a rose-colored chair illuminated by recessed lights took center stage. A steel stool on wheels in the corner of the small room looked clinical enough to be for Dr. Randall. El stopped in the opposite corner, in front of a flowered chair that had seen better days.

"So, I sit here?" I pointed at the chair that reminded me of a dentist's office, without the strange metal devices.

The hypnotist gestured once again, palm up, to my chair before she turned to El. "If you would please stay very quiet."

El nodded. She usually was a good sport. Besides, if she deserted me, I wouldn't have let her live it down since going to the hypnotist was her idea. She took her seat as I took mine.

Dr. Randall started adjusting my chair. "Tell me when it feels right for you."

I nodded. My pulse pounded in my ears. It took me a while to relax even in my favorite doctor's office, let alone here. As the shadowed ceiling came into view, I noticed its pink color, a slightly darker shade than the walls—or maybe the color only looked different because of the lighting. The chair stopped moving.

"Lie back," Dr. Randall said.

I tried to relax the way I did with Dr. Venkatesan. I pictured his smiling face. If I quit smoking, he would be so pleased.

"Close your eyes and listen to my voice."

It wasn't hard to follow her instructions. After a moment, music started playing; it sounded like a beautiful summer day. Water was running somewhere while fresh green leaves rustled above me. Not too far away, the songs of birds lulled me to sleep. Dr. Randall talked softly, telling me to relax my hands and feet, then the rest of my body. When I took yoga, my instructor had used the same technique at the end of our classes. The strange chair I was sitting in seemed to melt away.

"Your friend will sleep through our session without following my suggestions, and you will both wake up at the end of the hour."

I smiled, floating in that green world under a brilliant blue sky.

Dr. Randall spoke again, her voice calm yet commanding. "You are in control of your own destiny. You will not smoke again."

I snorted. She didn't believe the hypnotic suggestion would work for me. The destiny thing was absolutely not true. The world never cared what I wanted. If it had, Harry would still be alive.

I fidgeted. The running water was starting to make me uncomfortable. I might need a restroom soon, but I imagined it would be hard to get up when I couldn't feel my legs.

"I want to talk to that inner part of you."

Someone woke up deep inside me. I stopped listening to the water. The numbness of my body didn't keep me from questioning the command. A door opened, and a cell phone beeped out a tune. That new part of me knew the Bach fugue. Dr. Randall's stool squeaked, and the music started again.

I couldn't see El, but I could hear her breathing through her mouth, not snoring like I would have done. She probably fell asleep in her comfy chair, her head fallen gently to the side. I guess the music hadn't disturbed her.

From the other room, I heard a voice. That person inside me struggled to come to the surface. His thoughts were much sharper than mine.

Who is talking in that room? You must try to concentrate, he whispered.

Why*?* I asked even though the voice was hard to resist. If I could move my legs—or any part of my body—I would have left the chair. Struggling, I finally managed to open my eyes for a moment, catching a glimpse of a fuzzy pink blob and another darker one.

You must focus, this presence inside me said. He still hadn't said why. Had I missed something? Dr. Randall's voice was pitched much higher than before; I heard the word privacy. The other figure said something unintelligible.

Suddenly, a sharp noise made my ears ring.

The pink blob fell to the floor, and everything went black.

Chapter 2

When I woke up, the room was full of men. I was glad I'd worn jeans instead of a skirt. The bright light from two portable lamps that hadn't been here before, made me blink. What was going on?

"Come on Sissy, wake up." El leaned over me, her face not as attractive as I remembered. Her exaggerated brown cheeks trapped her cute nose as if I was looking at a closeup on a webcam. "The police are here."

"I'm awake." Was the hour over? A flash exploded, and blue spots stuck to my vision even after I shut my lids. Heaven help me, did somebody take a picture of me while I was under? I imagined my chubby face on a bulletin board in a room full of young studs.

You should exercise. It's good for the brain, as well as the body.

So, I hadn't imagined the voice.

"Who are you?" I said aloud, followed by a string of expletive-deletive swear words—another bad habit I'd picked up since Harry passed away.

My fellow students at Oxford would never believe this!

"Don't you know who I am?" El cried out. Tears ran down her face. "I should never have talked you into coming here."

"I recognize you." I propped myself up and swung my legs to the side a little too fast. The room flew around me until I managed to concentrate enough to make it stop.

I however, do not know you or should I say we?

"I'm Sissy Holmes," I said before silently cursing myself for talking aloud again.

"I know who you are." El wiped the tears from her face and turned to speak to a man in a dark blue uniform beside her. "Something is terribly wrong."

He took out a small flashlight that I promptly batted away.

"Is she always this difficult?" the man asked.

El shrugged. I'd never known she thought I was difficult. Did I fuss all the time?

You are well-advanced in years. The voice spoke again before I could stand up for myself like any self-respecting sixty-two-year-old should,

"It's time you told me who you are."

El shot me a horrified look.

"I mean I know who you are," I said before pointing at the guy who tried to shine a light in my eyes. "Who's that?"

"He's an EMT, you know, an ambulance attendant." El produced a couple of tissues from her pocket and dabbed at her nose.

"What happened to Dr. Randall?" I asked.

"She's been shot," a man standing in the doorway said.

The game is afoot.

El's sobs shook her slim shoulders as she turned to the wall away from prying eyes. Her need for privacy made me look away. You must think you're Sherlock Holmes or something. This time, I remembered not to talk out loud and let my response echo in my thoughts.

Indeed, I am. And my dear lady, your birth surname is the same as mine. I wonder if we are related?

You're a fictional character. You don't exist, I thought back.

I do not feel fictional. I feel very real, but where have I been? The last thing I remember is being very old.

Even after he stopped talking, I felt his presence. Hearing voices had to qualify me for a little cup of pills and a nice soft bed.

"I guess you had a hard time waking me up," I said and glanced around the room starkly defined by the new lights. Even the chair where El had slept was more faded than I remembered. In the brightness, the roses trapped between the thin blue lines on the beige background appeared more apricot than pink. "How is Dr. Randall?"

"She's dead." El came back to my side. She wiped more tears away with a handful of tissues. "Are you okay? I guess you were still hypnotized when everything happened."

Afraid to speak, I nodded. El was upset enough without me telling her there was a voice in my head that most definitely shouldn't be there. Let alone that it said it was Sherlock bloody Holmes.

Dr. Randall was dead. Thinking the words didn't make them any more believable.

A fairly tall man stood in the doorway wearing a khaki raincoat you might expect one of those old-time P.I.'s to wear. All he needed was a fedora to look the part of an old black-and-white film character. He'd been staring at El, but now his gaze shifted to me.

"Did you hear anything?"

After pulling myself together, I told him how, at first, I couldn't open my eyes because the hypnotist had told me to close them. How Dr. Randall went into the other room to answer her cell phone. "I guess I fainted after this loud noise."

"Do you remember what she said?" He wasn't a bad-looking man, sporting thick salt-and-pepper hair and a bit of stomach hanging over his belt. His blue eyes were warm enough, so I guess I didn't seem so bad myself.

Please do not hypothesize about a man's likes and dislikes without giving me the opportunity to withdraw.

Ignoring this sign of insanity, I tried to remember what Dr. Randall had said. I shook my head.

I remember, Sherlock whispered. His thoughts appeared in my brain in such an orderly way, I was thoroughly fascinated. How could he remember something when I couldn't? Not saying stuff out loud was hard.

If you would focus, he said before I started to interrupt him.

Then something even stranger happened.

He talked, using my voice. "I did hear Dr. Randall say the word privacy."

"Someone must have wanted her files," the detective said, writing in his small black notebook. His fancy slim silver pen might have been a Christmas present from a girlfriend. "What about the other person?"

I felt my mouth again after a subtle shift. "Before my eyes closed, I only saw a blur, as if they were standing in the dark. I thought the fuzzy pink figure was Dr. Randall because of the color of her clothing."

The detective nodded and wrote something else.

"Can you give me your phone numbers so I can follow up with you?" He looked down at his notebook as if avoiding my gaze.

El handed him her card. He gave her one of his own and pushed two into my hand, along with a pen. I wrote my name and number on the back and returned it to him. It would have been easier if he'd written it down himself.

"I hate to interrupt, but if you don't need my help?" The EMT held his bag as if he was ready to sprint out the door. A lady, also dressed in a dark blue uniform, hovered behind him.

"Thanks so much," El said, "we're fine."

She studied me as if trying to decide if that was true before handing me a tissue. "To wipe your hands. They took your fingerprints when you were still under."

Glancing down I saw that my hands were a mess. El held up her hands, and there were shadows of the ink on her fingertips. When I scrubbed at my own hands, I found that I couldn't get all the ink off either.

"Do you feel okay?"

I wondered if she thought I needed a psychiatrist. Even when my grief had swallowed me whole, I still hadn't gone to a shrink. But then again, people aren't supposed to hear voices in their head. I must be crazy now.

Sherlock interrupted again. *I want to look at the hypnotist's office.*

Ignoring him, I let El help me stand. Tomorrow would be soon enough to find myself some help. It wasn't fair. Multiple personality disorder had to be a serious condition. I'd seen a movie where a lady named Eve had all these different people inside her. She didn't always know what she'd done which seemed wrong.

As we walked out of the office, Sherlock told me that he certainly agreed that her doctors must have been very gullible.

What was wrong with me? I'd never heard voices before today.

There is a more logical reason for my existence.

You don't say, I responded before remembering to get back to reality.

I sighed. El and I stepped into the shadowed elevator. Getting away from the lights and people was a welcome change. Everyone, even El, had known what was going on—everyone except me.

Before Sherlock said anything more, I mentally pushed him away and concentrated on putting one foot ahead of another until we were outside the building.

Four police cars had parked diagonally in front of the sidewalk, blocking our direct route to the street. Then we had to walk around the orange cones that marked the pile of broken cement where the construction guys had been working. El held onto my arm.

It is a conundrum, I admit. Talking to you is not what I would have expected in any scenario. My fellows at Oxford would have been interested in our situation.

Walking to the car took all my concentration. After El unlocked her Mini, she took my elbow again. This had gone far enough. I pushed the presence in my mind back and prepared an expletive-deletive to say to my friend.

"Really," I said aloud and stopped when I saw her face. She had that startled why-are-you-yelling at me look that I'd only seen a few times before. I wanted to tell her to knock it off, but I didn't. "I appreciate your help. But what gives?"

"They think we had something to do with her murder."

If I'd taken a good look at El before, I would have seen how upset she was. Her lowered brow made the slight lines at the corners of her eyes deeper, and her mouth was missing her usual half-smile.

"Why?" I asked. "I couldn't get out of that chair when the cell phone beeped out Bach. But I heard you snoring over in the corner." A snort of disbelief came out of me before I remembered Sherlock. He seemed too refined to appreciate a woman who could do a decent snort.

My friend pulled a tissue from her pocket to dab her nose again. She looked very refined. If you put El in a long dress and stacked her hair on top of her head, she could easily pass for a Victorian lady. "The receptionist said she didn't see anyone else come into the office."

"I didn't see any receptionist, only beige chairs and those funny pictures."

El hadn't taken charge as she normally did, at least not as much. I was glad she didn't say anything about me acting like a fool.

"I guess the receptionist sat behind that mirror. That's what the detective said. She told Dr. Randall when the patients came into the waiting room. The doctor liked to greet them herself."

"You had quite a conversation." I wondered why she was so worried. Dr. Randall might have given her a suggestion too, except everything that I remembered had been said to me. I snorted again when I pictured the doctor talking about my destiny. Except weren't my eyes closed when that happened?

"More like an interrogation," El snapped. "It was very unpleasant."

"Hey, Dr. Randall didn't say much to me. How do we know the receptionist was behind the mirror?" I dropped into the low car seat of her Mini too fast; blood rushed to the top of my head. I closed my eyes.

"Are you okay?" El's voice came from the darkness forcing me to partially open my eyes.

"I'll be fine," I said closing my eyes again. It was embarrassing to be so feeble. "Why don't we go home?"

"Yes, that would be best."

After El closed her door, I opened my eyes again. The temperature was in the sixties, warm for Veterans Day. It didn't matter now if it was a national holiday since El and I had both retired from the Federal service. We still made plans, however, for every national holiday like we did before.

Beside me, El's shoulders shook as if she was cold. I shivered too when I thought about what had happened while we were both out of it.

Only a few feet away from us, someone had shot my hypnotist.

Murder was not something that happened in places like Bethesda, Maryland, at least not very often. Whoever killed Dr. Randall could have killed us too.

"Have you ever seen a dead body outside of a funeral home?" El didn't turn to look at me. Her eyes were glued to the road.

"Only Harry's." Our jobs at the Food and Drug Administration hadn't been clinical ones. We'd only set-up the panels for the doctors to discuss new medical devices, intraocular lenses and such that had been submitted for approval. No one had ever insisted that we look at dead bodies. My degrees were in chemistry because I'd barfed in high school when my pithed frog flexed his leg.

Sherlock had to add his input. *I've seen a dead body, many of them. Dr. Watson inspected most of them in our investigations.*

"When I suggested you go to a hypnotist. I thought it would help." El's voice trembled as if she might have a real crying jag coming on.

"There was no way you could have known what would happen." I closed my eyes but opened them again when I couldn't stop imagining the bright red stain on Dr. Randall's fuzzy pink suit.

Day Two
Chapter 3

The next morning, I felt terrible after brushing my teeth and doing all the normal things. My condo smelled stuffy, too. The glass door to the balcony made a grinding noise when I shoved it open to let the November air in. That's when it hit me. I hadn't had a cigarette since yesterday morning!

My nose started running as if I was coming down with a cold. When I swallowed a couple of aspirins in the bathroom, my throat felt sore which might be why I didn't want to light up. Maybe the hypnotist *had* been the solution to my smoking problem. Unfortunate that she was also quite dead. She'd been nice. The news might have the latest developments if I remembered to turn on the TV tonight.

There had been music, the doctor's voice, and a noise. Something else lurked in my groggy mind, but it refused to come to me.

I read my email and sipped coffee which I had deleted from my work routine years ago. I started drinking it again after my retirement. El had suggested it would help me stay awake a decent amount of the day instead of taking the afternoon naps I'd been enjoying at the time.

I trashed most of the messages in my inbox, except for one unread e-mail from El. She'd asked me to go to the Smithsonian with her this Friday. Today. I'd never responded yesterday, and she hadn't reminded me as we drove to my appointment with the hypnotist.

A trip to the Smithsonian didn't sound fun. Before I went in the kitchen to clean up, I pecked out a negative response to El telling her I didn't feel like going.

I shuddered when I thought how I'd acted like a fool in front of the policemen. El was used to me acting weird. She had a way of never bringing up those times when I couldn't act normal (at least for me) after Harry died.

The police were probably reading Dr. Randall's files right now.

For the first time, I wondered what El had told the poor doctor. She might have told her how I swore all the time. I'd come up with some interesting strings of expletive-deletives lately. Or she could have told her how I'd smoked a cigarette in the bathroom of the Smithsonian and every other non-smoking high-class joint in Washington, D.C. Did she think I needed medication for my depression? She had suggested I go to a therapist before. The only difference this time was that Dr. Randall was also a hypnotist.

I didn't want anyone to know the details of Harry's death or how much I missed him. My feeble mind had assumed I was getting better. Obviously not. I'd retired six months later because people at work kept giving me I'm-so-sorry looks.

The familiar clink of clean dishes straight out of the dishwasher reminded me of Harry too. I turned around to yell at him about leaving dishes in the sink. Of course, he wasn't sitting in his recliner reading the morning news.

The morning Harry died I'd known he was gone right away. El couldn't understand when I told her that he no longer looked like my Harry. If he'd been anyone else, I think his body would have creeped me out. Even so, I couldn't bear to see him again at the funeral home.

Other people asked me why his casket wasn't open. El didn't ask. We'd never been close in the ten years we worked in the same division at the Food and Drug Administration. I appreciated her standing beside me that day more than I can say. My only close family, my aunt and uncle, were negotiating a deal for their import/export business in Hong Kong. My sister-in-law and her mother had never been that fond of me. And our friends had been couples. I didn't fit in any longer, even at my own husband's funeral.

If it hadn't been for El, I don't know if I would've survived those first months. She bought me groceries and talked to me when all I could do was growl. Only El knew what happened the day Harry died too. I didn't tell anyone else—not even Aunt Pet.

Your friend does not seem to be indiscreet.

Oh no! I had heard a voice yesterday, one that supposedly belonged to a fictional character. "I need a doctor, a real doctor."

You are not crazy. I do exist, he insisted.

It must be a joke.

"Okay, come out whoever you are!"

No one popped up to show their face from behind my teal sofa or the chairs that decked my white brick fireplace. Cold air poured into the living room. I walked over to close the door, but instead walked out onto the balcony.

"El, enough," I said. No one was there.

You are talking to yourself, he said.

"I need help." Five stories below my balcony, the parking lot was only half-full. It's not like I wanted to jump. Why was I looking at the ground?

I want to visit the scene of the crime. Also, you should call me Mr. Holmes or at least Sherlock.

The compulsion felt like how I wanted a cigarette after being stuck in a meeting for hours, only stronger. Sherlock desperately wanted to go back to Dr. Randall's office. My body jumped into motion putting on my coat, taking my purse and jacket off the pegs by the door. Before I could decide that I didn't want to go, we were out of my condo and in the elevator on our way down to the underground parking garage.

"Now, stop this. You can't just make me do things."

I do apologize. However, I think you'll agree that we should go as soon as possible.

"They won't let us in her office," I said although I was intrigued. An attractive man from the floor below mine was standing by his black Volvo several rows away. I waved at him as if talking to myself was the most normal thing in the world.

We must try. Do you still have the detective's card?

I put it into my purse yesterday, I thought before I slipped inside my car.

If you, or should I say we, and Miss El are suspects. We should move swiftly to find out who had a motive to murder this Dr. Randall. I do not put much trust in the constabulary. In my experience, puzzles are beyond them.

"The detective didn't seem so bad."

My alter ego didn't answer for a change.

Before today, I'd never felt uncomfortable in my red Focus. When I looked at the passenger seat, I expected to see Sherlock Holmes putting a finger on the side of his nose like a hound on the scent. My unease turned to alarm on the Beltway when he didn't want me to take the Connecticut ramp instead of waiting for the ramp to Wisconsin Avenue. Of course, he didn't know that I could cut across to Wisconsin Avenue on Jones Bridge Road. I waited for the Wisconsin ramp. It didn't really matter.

It took us over half an hour to drive to the hypnotist's office; I parked in the lot half a block away. He took over again when we were outside the building. Sherlock was a fast learner in his new role, opening the door, propelling us across the marble entryway into the elevator where we pushed number four. We were standing in front of the door to her office when he hesitated.

What does this yellow tape mean?

"It means that no one is supposed to go inside her office because it's a crime scene." I hadn't even finished speaking when my hand reached out and twisted the knob. The door swung inward, leaving the tape along the crack. We could smooth it over the door later.

I don't suppose you have a gun in your bag.

"Of course not," I said wondering if Victorian women had revolvers in theirs. When I had time, I'd have to do a search online to see if revolvers had been around in the Victorian era.

Why was the door unlocked? Surely, they must lock the doors to crime scenes. We paused in the waiting room full of pictures of rats in human clothes.

Someone else has been here.

The two-way mirror had to be unethical. Out of the corner of my eye, I saw a flash of color as if someone moved quickly past the door beyond the pink treatment room.

They are still here. Sherlock, still in control of my body, moved forward as if ready to spring and tackle the interloper.

I wanted to leave, not particularly excited about adding myself to the Maryland crime statistics.

This may be our chance to discover a critical bit of information. We can leave whoever is inside undisturbed.

Before I could stop him, Sherlock walked me—us—into the pink treatment room and crouched behind the rose-colored chair. I agreed to stay for a few minutes as long as we didn't move any closer. At least the chair made for a good hiding spot. I prepared to assert myself when someone turned on the lights.

A red-haired man stood in the doorway to Dr. Randall's office.

"What are you doing here?" he asked in a high-pitched voice that belied his six-foot frame. He frowned as if he didn't expect to sound that way.

"I'm one of the women who was here yesterday when it happened. And you, I suppose, are with the police?" I improvised.

He glanced back at the office. "No, I'm her husband. The police asked me to meet them with the spare keys to her files. They're late."

I'd been planning on using my small purse as a weapon—not that it would do much to a man his size. If that were to be my only weapon however, it would need a couple of rolls of quarters for extra weight. I decided to play the role of a weak female instead of an avenging angel.

Sherlock was no good to me. I imagined him sitting in a cozy chair by the fire puffing away on his... No, we'll have none of that.

A strange look must have passed over my face. Mr. Randall frowned, as if he was suddenly suspicious of me. "What's wrong?"

A scene from my favorite PBS show flashed through my mind. The young female detective saw a change in the person before her. That's when she realized she shouldn't have come alone. I wondered if I'd made the same mistake. Except for his muscular physique, he hadn't look dangerous.

"I was thinking how terrible you must feel," I lied then grabbed the arm of the chair and pulled myself up, hoping Mr. Randall wouldn't look as tall if I rose. Could he have killed his wife? My mental visitor interrupted my thoughts.

I imagine it's wise not to tell him I'm here.

In the Victorian sitting room, my detective had one of those angular faces that the old film versions sported. Had Sherlock been a real person?

Dr. Randall's husband walked back into the office and picked up some keys from the desk. I thought he must be younger than his wife, but his red hair, much thinner near his crown, made him look older.

He looked over his shoulder, silhouetted against the morning sunshine. "I don't think it's sunk in yet. I keep expecting her to come through the door asking me why I'm in her office."

"You're not a hypnotist, too?" My voice was probably too loud. But I was determined to take control.

That is brilliant, my dear. We need to know more about him.

Mr. Randall pushed his black glasses up his nose. "I'm an accountant."

He didn't look like an accountant—or a killer. Was it an act? If he had killed his wife, I could be his next victim.

"Why don't you sit down?" Mr. Randall said, pointing to the chair behind him. He looked directly into my eyes without flinching.

A representative from a medical device company that I'd known at work could say anything with a straight face. He'd fooled me a couple of times until I realized I wasn't that good at judging people. I stayed behind the chair.

"Are you sure the police won't mind? I know I shouldn't have come into the office since it's a crime scene."

He didn't seem to have a weapon, but perhaps he didn't need one. The man looked strong enough to snap me in two if he wanted.

Compose yourself, my resident detective said. He was right. False bravado might keep the man in check.

"I'm Sissy Holmes."

"My name is Harvey Randall."

We stared at each other until the front door opened.

"Mr. Randall?" a voice said from the waiting room.

"We're in here," The red-haired man said, not taking his eyes from mine.

Walk into the office.

I started to respond that I didn't think that was a good idea when my body walked around the pink chair. Mr. Randall silently let me pass.

What do you see?

A wide, light-colored oak desk with a dark rose-colored leather chair placed parallel to the window, two matching visitor chairs in front, one toppled. All the shiny surfaces were covered with a dark powder. The doctor, when sitting at her desk, had faced the middle of the room instead of the window. Sunlight streamed through the white plantation blinds. One slat was broken.

A row of nine pink file cabinets filled most of the opposite wall which had also been dusted with the dark powder.

Two plants of the trailing variety topped the cabinets, one bright green, the other variegated. Three framed degrees hung above them. The largest one was from Johns Hopkins University, a Doctoral degree, placed in the middle with a degree from Mississippi, and a Bachelor of Science on the left. A degree from Wisconsin, Master of Science was hung on the right.

A collection of snow globes peeked out of the vines crisscrossing the tops of the file cabinets. Some of the globes had city names: San Francisco, Philadelphia, and Oklahoma City.

Directly in front of the door to the hall, yellow tape outlined the shape of a body. Her legs were extended as if the doctor had tried to run away before she bled a blotch two-feet wide. The other darkened red spots on the file cabinets and the floor grew from pinpoints to the size of half dollars close to where her body fell. I shuddered when I thought of her walking to her desk. The bullet that killed her had no trouble penetrating the bulky pink tweed she'd worn yesterday, or ripping through her lung and perhaps an artery close to her heart.

Very good. I do think you are correct. She walked across the room to get something from her desk when her assailant shot her.

A phone and two coffee cups (pink, of course) sat on the desk. The cups read *Dr. Phillipa Randall, serving your health needs* with a phone number starting with 215 in blue. There was another door in the corner which I supposed went to the receptionist's office. More certificates were on the wall on the other side of the desk, next to the file cabinets. The door to the hallway was opposite the windows.

Keep looking, even a trifle can be important, Sherlock said.

Pink paper in a rose-colored leather box, a matching cup with a gold embossed design holding black pens, a snow globe with the name Dallas held up by a miniature city skyline, and a burgundy file completed my inventory of the items on her desk. When I leaned forward, I saw "Sissy Carpenter" typed neatly on a strip of paper inserted into the folder's clear tab.

If you are worried, you could ascertain what's inside the folder.

My own personal ghost sounded amused.

I didn't need to look. El was discreet. Our former jobs at the FDA had trained us to only release necessary information. It was the forever deviling red-tape of working in a bureaucracy that had made me paranoid. I had spent a good deal of time at work trying to figure out what new problems would appear on my desk. Even though I'd retired over a year ago, I was only now starting to understand how much the job had affected me.

"What are you doing here?" a voice said with a slight southern twist. I recognized the detective right away even if he were only a dark shape in the doorway to the treatment room with the rose chair behind him. "What are you doing here?" he asked again.

"It was so unbelievable, I had to take a look for myself." That much was true.

His expression changed which made me think he might believe me. He pointed to the room with the rat people. "Wait for me. I want to talk to you before you leave."

I wanted to ignore him and make a quick exit, but I didn't. Dr. Randall's death was very real to me now, and a murderer was on the loose.

Chapter 4

When the detective let me pass, I caught a whiff of my old friend, Mr. Tobacco. *Do you suppose I always smelled that way to other people?* I thought before cursing under my breath. If I kept talking to Sherlock, he would never go away.

Had I studied the tobaccos of your time, I'm sure I would've been able to tell you the name. The smell from this detective is unfamiliar to me.

I didn't realize before I sat down that a spot above my right eye had begun to pulse in a really irritating kind of way; almost as irritating as Sherlock's voice. I put a hand to my forehead and held down the twitching muscle.

You were wise not to touch your folder. The detective might have misconstrued why you were concerned about its contents.

Then why did you suggest I look? I didn't wait for his answer. My glance strayed to the picture of a small town that was celebrating a holiday directly across from my chair. Red, white, and blue buntings hung from the railing of the gazebo where a band of rats tooted away on tubas, trumpets, and flutes. In front of the gazebo, a round gray-haired rat spoke to a policeman in a tall hat like the ones I'd seen in old movies. I reached into my purse and pulled out the detective's card. *This is your fault since you made me come here*, I directed at Sherlock.

On the contrary, we needed to see the scene of the crime. What is the name on the card? I don't think he ever introduced himself.

Thomas Kirkland, Detective was printed in bold black letters across the middle. A blue logo for the Montgomery County Police was embossed in the upper left-hand corner and phone numbers appeared in the opposite and lower right-hand corner.

As a consulting detective, you will need to earn the local constabulary's respect, Sherlock whispered as if someone might hear. *However, I do prefer working alone—or at least alone with my Watson.*

"I don't want to investigate a murder," I mumbled.

We will need to become a bit chummy with those doing the official inquiry if we are to make sure that you and Miss El are no longer suspects.

This voice, this aberration, ignored me. I was crazy, and Sherlock Holmes did not exist. That was all.

Are you not curious?

The murder of Dr. Randall had nothing to do with me. We would only get in the way. Sherlock didn't respond.

El was worried though. I'd seen fear in her eyes, or had it been guilt for insisting I go to the hypnotist? When she first suggested it, I assumed she'd picked the best available hypnotist. So, why had El been afraid to be hypnotized herself?

I wasn't used to finding flaws in my friend. I had always thought she was too much of a perfectionist in her personal life and, ironically, too quick to jump into things. Once she found out about my newest problem, she certainly wouldn't feel comfortable around me. But I didn't want to think what my life would be like without her.

You are not giving Dr. Randall enough credit. She was a well-educated woman. Not that such abilities cannot be put to disreputable use. I have experience with such villains. You yourself said that she seemed a nice woman.

Nice people don't get themselves murdered—at least that's what I'd always assumed.

Of course, many victims in my time were scandalous themselves. Yet, I was not typically called in to investigate. Greed, jealousy, anger drive some to murder the innocent without regret.

I couldn't take my eyes off the picture closest to me. Two little rat boys dressed in green striped shirts and dungarees, ducked around the white gazebo with one of them carrying a gold pocket watch. They must have stolen the watch from the mayor who patted his empty vest pocket. These pictures were detailed enough to keep people busy as they waited.

A few minutes later, Mr. Randall wordlessly walked past me and out the door. Detective Kirkland followed only pausing to turn on another light before facing me.

"Mr. Randall said that he opened the door before you arrived. Guess that takes care of the breaking and entering or disturbing a crime scene charges. Haven't you ever heard of the criminal returning to the scene of his crime? Do you want to be a suspect?" He sat down heavily in the chair next to me, tucking his coat down inside the smooth wooden arms.

"Of course not. I didn't touch a thing," I said, looking at the rat picture again. In the crowd of spectators, seated on lawn chairs in front of the gazebo, two more rat boys raced down an aisle, one of them carrying a yellow purse with pink spots.

"I'm surprised you didn't look in your own folder."

I dragged my attention to the detective beside me. His blue eyes held mine so long that I noticed a spot in his left eye, a slice of green iris.

"I was tempted."

"I brought the warrant for the files. This was your first visit?"

He must have looked in the folder and seen that I wanted to quit smoking. I nodded, wondering if he thought I was mentally ill. "I came to Dr. Randall so she could help me quit smoking."

The detective's dark bushy eyebrows shot up accentuating his eyes. Maybe he hadn't read my file after all. With the cabinets locked and my file being the only one on her desk, I was impressed he hadn't violated my privacy or maybe he was completely incompetent.

"You quit smoking yesterday?"

"Day One." As if on cue, my nose began to run. "There are side effects," I said, pulling a tissue from my purse. My pack of long cigarettes that I'd wanted to smoke yesterday was in plain view.

"I'm jealous," he said and took out his notebook. "How did you find Dr. Randall?"

He must have asked El the same question and wondered if I knew Dr. Randall before I was her patient. She could be a friend from school except that I'd never been to the state of Mississippi and never attended Wisconsin. I suppose that I could have run into her ten years ago at Hopkins when I was teaching a class in the Public Policy program. I shook my head. No, nothing made sense.

He frowned pulling my attention back to him. "You're not going to tell me?"

"Oh, it's not that. I was trying to think of a reason I might want to kill her—hypothetically of course. I only met Dr. Randall yesterday." Acting dumb was becoming a habit.

The detective nodded.

At least he understood why I agreed to the appointment, even if El told him I'd argued with her about going into the hypnotist's office. As a smoker himself, Kirkland would know how hard it was to quit.

"What's the receptionist's name?" Sherlock blurted out using my voice.

"Jessica Clayborn." The detective frowned as if he had someone talking to him, too. "Why do you want to know?"

"Well, this hidden receptionist thing is weird. Nobody could see her, yet she says she was there the whole time." I was sure she'd ducked out to meet a friend or have a cigarette.

"That thought did occur to me, but you are not to act like an amateur sleuth." At first, his voice sounded too loud until it dropped in volume. "You're not a private investigator, are you?"

"I am a consulting detective," Sherlock said before I could stop him. "I've *thought* about becoming a consulting detective," I added.

Kirkland scowled as if he expected as much. "If you don't have a license, I could arrest you." He'd been friendly before. The look on his face made me understand that he would have no scruples about locking me away. If I kept talking to a fictional character that might be a good thing.

What do I have to do to convince you that I am real, my dear lady?

I did my best to ignore Sherlock. Kirkland studied my face.

"You're the one that scared my best friend and made her think that we were your number one suspects," I reminded him.

"You were there when the murder happened," he said without blinking.

The casual way he'd agreed to talk to me had made me think that El was wrong.

He was trying to make you relax, see if you would tell him a piece of information that you would not otherwise say. Lulling the suspect into a false sense of security is a common interrogation technique.

If I'd been guilty, that could have been a serious mistake. "What did the receptionist say she was doing?"

"She was sure that no one came into the reception area after you two arrived. And Dr. Randall always kept the back door locked." He flipped through the pages of his notebook. "The doctor never let anyone in during an appointment. She was very careful and kept the back door and file cabinets locked." he paused, flipping through the pages again, "you said you heard a cell phone in the office when Dr. Randall was sitting beside you in the treatment room and then voices."

"I'm pretty sure I did. She did this relaxation thing, and I had the hardest time opening my eyes after I was hypnotized."

Kirkland raised one eyebrow. He wouldn't have believed anyone who believed in hypnotism. I didn't blame him. When we first arrived at Dr. Randall's office, I hadn't believed in hypnotism either.

"Come on," he took my arm and pulled me into the treatment room. "Stand here." He walked to the desk. "What do you see?"

"Where Dr. Randall was standing yesterday." What had I missed when I'd looked at the room with Sherlock?

"The room is very bright." He flipped through his notebook again. "You told me it was like they were standing in the dark."

"It's not fair for you to compare what I see now with what I saw while I was hypnotized."

On that we do agree.

I guess Sherlock wanted me to understand that he could not see more than I could, even under hypnosis.

"I wish I could tell you why. Maybe I'll be able to remember more in a couple of days." Being cooperative had seemed like a good idea. Kirkland still didn't look like he believed me. The more I said, the more his disbelief seemed to grow.

They look for the most obvious solution, Sherlock said.

On the way home, I thought about looking for a psychiatrist. I was sure that I was our detective's number one suspect. If I continued to hear voices in my head, there was no telling what I might have done. The only consolation I had was that if they charged me, I could always plead insanity.

Day 3
Chapter 5

"I can't believe you went without me," El said when I showed up at her condo the next morning. Sherlock hadn't thought of her when he decided to go to the hypnotist's office.

Neither did you, he reminded me.

He was right, which made me feel even more guilty. But if I hadn't gone to Dr. Randall's office when I did, the door would probably have been locked, and I wouldn't have met her husband. The doctor and the accountant didn't seem like a good match. She had appeared to be flamboyant, not afraid to do whatever she wanted even if that involved painting every room pink. Her husband, on the other hand, appeared more restrained. Maybe her willingness to expose herself to ridicule was a relatively new development? If I'd decided to start doing everything my own way, I don't think Harry would have been very happy.

Harry?

My husband, I thought and stopped before I said more. There was no need to explain Harry to Sherlock.

"Sissy?"

"Oh." I'd forgotten that I was talking to El. "Sorry about going without you."

"It was lucky that you went when you did." Bless her heart. She was good at seeing the bright side of things even when she disagreed with me.

I do not believe in luck. Sherlock couldn't seem to keep his thoughts to himself.

You don't exist so keep it down, I chastised him before I remembered I shouldn't even be answering. To El I said, "Yes, it worked."

She walked behind my chair and pulled out the cushion to fluff it. "What did you think of the husband?"

I leaned forward until she put the pillow behind me once more. Did I look that tired, so whipped that she thought I needed coddling?

"Well, I imagine the doctor had been the dominant personality in their relationship. He invited me into her office. The only thing he told me was that he was meeting the police so he could give them her keys."

I leaned back into the soft cushion. Yesterday had been exhausting, and my body—though not demanding a smoke every five minutes—was not happy; almost every part was stiff and achy. My head throbbed.

El had gone into her small kitchen. When she returned, she put a cup of black coffee on the glass-topped table in front of me. It perked me up right away.

"The detective doesn't believe us, does he?"

"When did you get that chair?" I said changing the subject, and pointed to the green chair where she was sitting. There was no reason to let her worry about what the detective might believe.

"Oh, must have been about six months ago." El took a sip of her own coffee before putting her cup down. "You haven't been here that much."

She'd told me last Christmas that she didn't want me to smoke in her condo unless I went out on the balcony. I'd felt a little betrayed by that. Ever since, I'd avoided coming to her place. El always agreed to meet me at our favorite restaurants or come over to my condo.

"How do you feel?" The way she was looking at me made me uncomfortable.

I felt like how Mr. Spock must have felt back on Vulcan after they put his soul back into his body. "As if I have a touch of the flu. Not too bad," I lied, not sure whether I liked my new self—the one with a built-in-detective, the one who lied to her best friend.

"It worked? You're not craving a cigarette?" El squinted as if she didn't believe me.

"You're the one that made the appointment."

She crossed her spotless beige-clad legs casually at the knee, one beige high heel shoe swinging while she sipped her coffee. El was more sophisticated than I could ever hope to be, and maybe more secretive. I looked down at my stained University of Maryland t-shirt.

A perfect Watson, my dear lady. I think she is an ideal friend.

El smiled. "You wanted to try everything,"

"Exactly. I'm surprised too. I haven't wanted to smoke at all," I said, wondering if I should tell her about Sherlock. My cursing was not my usual expletive-deletive. This one was twice as long.

El gave me a look as if I had said the curse out loud. "Did you ask about the receptionist's name? We need to talk with her. When we get a chance, I want to meet this husband, too." She took my cup. "You don't get to have all the fun."

"You didn't say you wanted to get involved before," I said following her into the kitchen. The black granite was clean as usual, uncluttered by dirty dishes or dishtowels flung on the countertop instead of hanging neatly from the handle of her dishwasher.

"Dr. Randall was someone we both knew." She took a swipe at the counter with a blue sponge. "Do you have any idea who might have killed her?"

"I don't know. What if we're nosing around, and the killer decides to add us to the body count?"

"Don't you want to investigate? It happened right under our noses." El slapped the damp sponge on the counter, sending droplets of water flying onto the shiny surface.

"What about the police? I ran into that detective at the office. You were right. He already has us on his list of suspects. He might even throw me in jail for interfering."

"What if he doesn't figure out who the real murderer is? As usual, you're thinking only of yourself."

I didn't tell her I had a defense. Maybe it wouldn't be so bad being locked in a cell.

"If you don't help me, I'll do it alone."

I could tell by the way she lowered her eyebrows that she would. El had always been a bulldog. Once she decided to do something, it was hard to make her stop. Her efforts to help me quit smoking had been exhausting. If I went with her, I might be able to keep her out of trouble.

"It's not going to be easy to find the receptionist only by her name. We don't know where she lives, or what directory to look in."

"I thought we should call Dr. Randall's office. The receptionist will be busy cancelling appointments and finding doctors for the other patients. Dr. Randall must have had regular patients that she didn't hypnotize."

"Do you have her number?" I was sure El only needed to pull out her little address book. She always kept it close at hand even though the information was also on her phone. The younger guys at the office had thought it was hilarious.

When we called, the receptionist answered right away. She agreed to meet us for lunch—our treat, of course. And she said something about paying for the services Dr. Randall performed yesterday. I wasn't sure that I should be paying for lunch or the medical bill since Dr. Randall had left me under hypnosis.

"Why are we always going out to eat?"

"Because that's what retired people do," El said.

I couldn't stop thinking about how I didn't want a cigarette. The doctor's suggestion must have done the trick with the regrettable creation of Sherlock. I didn't like him, or that the fact he seemed to have more control than I did. Except if he really was part of me, was I still in control? The whole thing was going to drive me crazy.

Only the most sympathetic person would even consider the possibility that I could exist, Sherlock said.

At least, I'd conquered my addiction to tobacco.

Chapter 6

Jessica Clayborn wasn't a surly girl with nose rings and heavy makeup; the young Goth woman I'd known at work hadn't been surly either. This Jessica Clayborn could have been one of those fussy middle-aged women who were always critical of everyone else. Maybe even an older woman, with a sharp nose and an even sharper tongue? But no. Our Ms. Clayborn was a small woman, maybe thirty years old, in a pink t-shirt with Nike written across it in glittery silver letters. Once she started to talk, I knew that she didn't match any of my receptionist stereotypes.

"I told them neither one of you was a likely suspect cause you were under hypnosis. They didn't understand." The small woman took a bite out of her cheeseburger at The Pit, a restaurant not far from Dr. Randall's office. The police hadn't said no when she asked to go into the office to cancel Dr. Randall's appointments.

"Have you ever been hypnotized?" El asked before she took a bite of her salad.

"Sure, I heard about her from a friend of mine. The Doc said therapy would be better for me than hypnotism. Cool, if only I'd had the money. She suggested I come work for her and gave me my sessions for free. I don't know what I would have done without her. I was just out of college and kept piling on the weight."

This doctor might have wanted to surround herself with people that she could control, Sherlock whispered, reflecting my own thoughts. Dr. Randall might not have been as nice as she appeared.

El gave me a look as if she could tell that I was having a conversation with myself. Would she be charged with murder too? I looked at my Cobb Salad and stabbed a chunk of chicken.

"Was Dr. Randall a good employer?" I asked.

"She liked to help people. Which I guess explains why she was so interested in hypnotism. I thought she might be taking it too far when she put in the treatment room. Worked for me, though, I guess. And lots of people want an easy way to quit smoking or eat less." She took another bite of her burger. "I still enjoy food, just never eat as much. Lost lots of weight after she hypnotized me."

She was very petite, maybe even a size zero. I stabbed a piece of lettuce this time. "It's hard to imagine you overweight."

Jessica laughed. "Once, I could have shown you pictures. But I burned the ones I didn't like. You know, erasing the past."

If only all of our mistakes were so easy to forget.

Even I have made mistakes.

El was staring at me again. I must've made a face. When I looked up, she switched her gaze to Ms. Clayborn. "Why were you so sure that no one came in the back door?"

"Wow, I don't think I said that to the police." The receptionist pushed her metal glasses back up her perky nose. "I told them she kept the door locked. Maybe she left it unlocked that day because she was expecting a visitor and didn't want to answer the door while she was with you."

Sherlock was anxious to comment. *Letting you think that she'd said the door was locked was probably another one of this detective's tactics. Dr. Randall obviously left it unlocked or someone was already in the office.*

"I already spoke to the detective about this." I watched her face, not sure what I expected to see. If she blushed or looked away, she might not be telling the truth.

She didn't do either. Still, that wasn't proof.

"I never left the office while you were there. If anyone else had been in the waiting room, I would've seen them," she said, looking directly at me before going back to El. There wasn't any change in the woman. Her voice was as steady as her gaze. I could have sworn she was telling us the truth.

That aspect of her story never bothered me Sherlock responded. *The placement of the rooms made it necessary for the murderer to walk past us if they entered by the waiting room which seems highly improbable.*

El took out a pad of paper and started writing. "Did anyone else come to the office earlier that day, someone who might have stayed in her office after their appointment?"

"No, she didn't have one of her regular appointments. Before you arrived, Rudolph Tessmeyer did come to talk to

Dr. Randall for a minute. I checked to see if he was gone after I saw you in the waiting room. He must have left her office through the back door." Ms. Clayborn looked at the cheeseburger and said, "I want to eat more."

The hypnotism didn't appear to eliminate the impulse, only one's ability to fulfill their desire. Maybe that's why I felt so bad. If I thought I had a very bad cold, I might not want to smoke, though it seemed real enough.

"Where is Mr. Tessmeyer from?"

"Oh, you know, Bethesda," she said, still staring at the cheeseburger.

"I did want to ask you about the hypnotism itself." I pushed my salad away and took a long drink of Diet Coke which was more satisfying.

"Ask away. Not sure I can help you."

"I'm wondering why I can't remember seeing Dr. Randall and whoever was with her." I tried again and couldn't see a face when I pulled up that memory.

Jessica leaned forward. "What did you see?"

"Just blurry shapes. There was this blob of pink which I imagine was Dr. Randall and a darker one beside her. I don't know why I can't remember seeing their faces."

"That is strange," she said, cocking her head to one side.

The waitress left the check. I slid a credit card into the black folder with the list of damages.

What are you doing? Sherlock asked. It was so hard to ignore him. Paying the bill, I responded. If I acted as if Sherlock was real, I didn't see much hope of banishing him.

What a strange practice. It does sound similar to when people kept accounts at their tailors or dressmakers. Many a dandy in the old days had trouble with such dealings.

When I looked up, El was staring at me again. She couldn't possibly know about Sherlock. I changed the subject. "Did Dr. Randall have any enemies?"

Jessica laughed. "Not unless you want to count Dr. Welker."

"Who's Dr. Welker?" El asked, jotting the information down.

"Another shrink on the same floor."

Jessica was still looking at her food. I sipped my Diet Coke.

Maybe he hadn't approved of her using hypnosis. I hadn't looked the doctor up in the Yellow Pages yet. My imagination had given Dr. Randall at least a half-page ad with quips such as "Trying to lose weight?" or "You can quit smoking in one visit."

"What about her friends?"

"The police asked me that too," Jessica paused. "I can't remember anyone. They hadn't lived here that long. They moved to the East Coast from Texas. Sorry, she didn't tell me much."

"This must be hard for you," El said in that socially acceptable way of hers.

"You didn't have to buy me lunch. I would have helped you anyway." Our new friend stood up. She looked very serious, her eyes focused, her mouth pursed. "I did like her. She was good to me when I needed a friend."

El and I stood too. I wasn't surprised when El gave her a hug. "What will you do?"

"I have a little money. I'll be fine until I find another job. My boyfriend wants me to move in with him." She smiled brilliantly.

"I'm happy for you," I said, and I *was*. Just because I didn't want a guy hanging around didn't mean that a thirty-year-old wouldn't.

"I have to go." Jessica gave me a hug which I wasn't prepared to receive. I tried to respond in kind.

"If you think of anything out of the ordinary..." I started to say.

"Let us know," El said finishing my sentence.

"I will. Don't worry about your bill. Your insurance will cover it. You know preventive medicine, that's for smoking cessation." She gave us a wave as she pushed through the revolving glass doors of the restaurant.

We sat down and waited for the waitress to return with my credit card.

"Dr. Welker shouldn't be hard to find."

"We need to talk to Rudolph Tessmeyer, too. He was there."

"We're still the best suspects." El wrote something else in her notebook before she looked up at me. "I mean, if we had a motive."

"That's why we need to figure out who wanted her dead." I shook my head.

Our detective has probably interviewed everyone on the floor by now to see if he can find a bit of information to steer him in the right direction, Sherlock added.

Whoever had killed Dr. Randall had walked right in and shot her in the middle of the day. My general instincts about people weren't always good, but I was pretty sure I'd be scratching her husband off my list. Mr. Randall hadn't seemed like the homicidal type.

In my experience, there is no such thing as a homicidal type unless you are referring to those that kill for the pleasure of it.

I blinked at my own stupidity. Of course, I wouldn't know a homicidal maniac from the next guy. I hoped I'd never run into one of those.

If we are dealing with such a creature, the police are the best-informed parties to confirm the killer's existence. During my lifetime, I was called upon to assist them with such cases. However, this murder strikes me as one of opportunity to carry out a single goal. Otherwise, they would not have taken the risk of being seen. The perpetrator will be someone connected to her.

I couldn't even guess who might have done it. Or imagine a situation where I would feel justified murdering someone.

Perhaps in self-defense or to protect another.

El had those little creases between her eyes. She looked as tired as I felt. Twelve hours of sleep might be enough to bring me back to fighting form. I'd need to be fit if I was going to investigate a murder. But I couldn't help feeling we should step back and let the detective do his work.

Day 4
Chapter 7

"What was his first name?" El pulled out her tablet and tapped the screen.

"Rudolph," I said. I picked up another piece of bacon while we ate at our favorite brunch spot, Tingalis. My Belgian waffle was waiting for an ocean of maple syrup. "Tell me why we're doing this again."

El moved her finger across the screen. "There are three R. Tessmeyers in Bethesda. Who would have thought?"

I hadn't slept well last night. If my refrigerator could talk, it would complain about how many times I'd viewed the contents without removing a thing. Nothing had looked good. I decided to give into my munchies this morning and not think about the healthy bowl of Cheerios El had ordered.

Why don't you let me handle this? I could feel Sherlock was anxious to take over my body.

Why had I suddenly gone nuts? I know I'd been down in the dumps for a long time. I thought I'd been getting better. After I retired, I'd settled into a more comfortable routine, even without Harry. My feelings hadn't changed. Lots of stuff reminded me of him, but now I remembered the bad times as well as the good. I was getting better at living without my husband. I'd had no crying fits for months. When I thought about him, I tried to imagine a big yellow caution sign with

Harry written boldly in black, my own little trick which worked most of the time.

Wouldn't it be nice if a big red stop sign suddenly popped up to remind me that I was going to say something that would upset people? I almost snorted a laugh when suddenly my master sleuth, my sign of crazy, took hold of the reins.

"Let's get started then," Sherlock said using my voice and grabbed my jacket from the back of the booth. He tossed my keys to El. "Why don't you drive?" I'd picked her up so she didn't have her car.

El grinned. "I thought you wanted to drive."

"Nonsense. If you drive, I will have time to think," Sherlock said.

I wanted to eat my breakfast.

Sherlock picked up my fork and stabbed two pieces of the waffle I'd cut up, stuffing them in our mouth.

El laughed and tossed some bills on the table. Was it just because she wanted to go? No, there was something else going on here. I decided to let my annoyance take a backseat for now. It wouldn't be long before we arrived at R. Tessmeyer's apartment.

The address belonged to a building that was one of those 1950s styles with windows in the corners of the pale stone facade. The maple trees in front still had most of their red leaves, making a nice contrast to the white building. After El hit the security button in the foyer, I heard a buzz as the door unlocked so we could go inside. This Tessmeyer was the first one listed in the phone book and lived on the sixth floor. If we were lucky, this one had also visited Dr. Randall's office the morning of her murder.

It felt strange when Sherlock controlled my body. His step was lighter than mine. We practically bounced down the sidewalk, leaving El to run after us. He was too energetic for my taste and should seriously get out of my head.

I was going to protest his extended control of my body, my expletive-deletive ready, when we found apartment 604. The Victorian detective rapped our knuckles on the door instead of using the bell visible to the right. A small label above it said R. Tessmeyer.

A small woman with a curved back appeared almost instantaneously. "You're not from the grocery. I know the boys from the grocery, and you're not any of them," she said walking away leaving the door open. "And who might you be?

El handed her one of her cards.

"We do apologize for the intrusion," Sherlock said. "Perhaps we could talk to you for a few minutes. Are you Mrs. Tessmeyer? Mrs. R. Tessmeyer?"

"Yes, that's me. Not many of us left, the Tessmeyers that is." She walked carefully across the dark blue Oriental carpet to a flowered, high-backed armchair by the window. She eased herself down and pulled a small pillow into the space for her lower back. "That'll do. Now out, both of you."

Mrs. Tessmeyer pointed to the six-paneled door that led to the hallway, as if she'd forgotten that she let us in.

Sherlock didn't let me budge an inch. "We're looking for a Rudolph Tessmeyer who might have gone to a Dr. Randall's office a few days ago."

"There are two of those. Why are you still here?" She glared at us under her neatly-combed page-styled gray hair.

El crossed the dark blue rug and headed for the door. Sherlock was fighting my efforts to follow her.

"My first initial is R too. R for the name Ruth. My son is named Rudolph, after his father. God rest his soul. And my grandson's name is also Rudolph, although he goes by the name Tommy because of his middle name. Never took too well to being called little Rudy. Can't say I blame him. I didn't want to saddle his father with the name, but my husband's parents insisted. They held the family money over our heads."

"You don't know which one might have had an appointment with Dr. Randall, do you?"

"Don't know, but this doctor's not an internist, is she?" the old lady said. "You girl, what are you doing in the hall?" Apparently, she'd changed her mind. El stepped back into the apartment, pulling the thick wooden door shut.

"Was she that woman on TV? Neither one of them would have chosen a female doctor, not for anything where they had to take off their clothes. Both stiff as a stick," Mrs. Tessmeyer said and laughed.

"We didn't want to upset you." Sherlock was still talking to the old woman even though our eyes were focused on a beautiful beige pitcher, copper-glazed on the lower half.

"Death doesn't upset me now—at least not my own." She chuckled. "Why do you want to talk to Rudy?"

"He was at the doctor's office the morning she was killed. We were wondering if he saw anything unusual." Sherlock moved our hand up to my mouth as if he was going to pull out his pipe before realizing what he was doing.

"I can tell you that as much as I love him, not likely he'd manage to kill someone. Doesn't have the stuffing for it. Especially not with a gun."

"Neither would we. I mean—shoot anybody," El stammered.

"And they're acting like you might have something to do with it?" She turned her head to the side and raised a darkly sketched eyebrow. "Not you, that's for sure. Now your friend—she could shoot someone," Mrs. Tessmeyer said, looking at me again.

Her gaze unnerved me almost as much as her comment. Sherlock took control again and strode over to the window. "Perhaps you would be so good as to tell us the correct address for your son?"

"That will be the house on Windsor Street," the old lady replied.

"Thank you so much for your help."

"You tell me what you figure out." The old lady's eyes were still focused on me.

Sherlock forced me to bow in her direction before he relinquished control. "Indeed."

Back in the elevator, El laughed. "You *are* acting strangely." She peered at my face, "Or should I be worried?"

I shook my head.

It was only 10:30 in the morning. Rudy's mother hadn't seemed to mind that we arrived on a Sunday. If they were Jewish, like so many others in this neighborhood, he might not mind either. Plenty of time to go visit this man and find out why he was seeing Dr. Randall. If I could get another ten hours of sleep, maybe when I woke up tomorrow, Sherlock would be gone.

Tessmeyer's house was only a few blocks away from his mother's apartment on one of those one-way Bethesda streets. The city had done its best to make it impossible for someone to drive around the block, some kind of traffic control I suppose. El parked three blocks away. We walked instead of circling around to his house again.

While we waited for Mr. Tessmeyer to answer the door, I admired the Tudor touches to his home. The windows had diamond-shaped panes with that dark leading you can see in stained glass windows at church. The black wrought iron fixtures must have been hard to find. The place was notably old even though the white stucco and brown wooden beams looked freshly painted.

A rather short, balding man with gold wire-rimmed glasses opened the door. "We don't allow door-to-door solicitation here."

El wedged herself into the door before it closed. "Mr. Tessmeyer? We're not selling anything. Your mother sent us." She was more aggressive than when we had talked to his mother.

"I suppose you better come in then," he said, stepping aside. The interior was dark except for the yellowish glow from a Tiffany-style lamp illuminating a brown leather recliner to one side of the red brick fireplace. He waved at a couch covered in a dark tapestry fabric—the only place to sit that wasn't covered by stacks of paper.

Sherlock took over again. "I understand that you saw Dr. Randall the day she died."

Tessmeyer was looking at the floor. "What does this have to do with my mother? Are you with the police?"

"We were there when Dr. Randall was killed." Sherlock talked as if he'd been given a divine right. I reminded him of his non-existence, trying to keep the wave of anger I felt under control. I would have smacked him if that was possible. Feeling so angry was unusual for me. Maybe Sherlock was the one who was angry.

Tessmeyer's shiny head popped up. He looked at me over his glasses. "Then you should already know I was gone before you arrived."

I took back control. There was no reason for me to be angry with Mr. Tessmeyer. "I'm having trouble remembering that day. I was hypnotized. Did you have an appointment?" I spoke quickly, hoping he would answer without thinking and Sherlock wouldn't interrupt.

He frowned. "No, I had to settle my account. I wasn't seeing her anymore."

I couldn't help wondering what had gone on between them. "Were you ever hypnotized by her?" As soon as I asked, I knew the answer.

His face became rigid. "I wanted to quit smoking, and the hypnotism worked," he said, relaxing for a moment before he frowned again, "with a few side effects."

"That's why I was there too. So far, it's worked."

I believe I know why he is so agitated. Indeed, if the same thing happened to me, I would be angry too.

"What were the side effects?" El asked, moving to the edge of her chair.

Mr. Tessmeyer jerked to his feet, startling my friend. "I'm really very busy. Why did you mention my mother?"

"She's fine," El said, leaning back on the firm cushion of the couch. "We talked to her first because she was listed as R. Tessmeyer in the phone book too."

"I'll thank you to leave her alone. She's in delicate health. And I'm busy, as I said." He motioned at the stacks of papers around the room. Sherlock made us pick up a paper from the ornately carved coffee table in front of the couch. I would never have invaded another person's privacy that way.

A consulting detective must sometimes take the initiative. It looks like he was selling stock, and from the total due, it was for a large number of shares.

"I'll thank you to leave," Tessmeyer said. He reached forward to take the sheet of paper, but Sherlock jerked it away.

"Are you having financial difficulties?" my sleuth asked. "This withdrawal is dated a few weeks ago."

"You should mind your own business." Mr. Tessmeyer took the paper from my hand and tumbled back into his chair. His slumped body made him appear much smaller.

"We just want to find out what happened," El said as she came to her feet. "Do you know who might have wanted to kill Dr. Randall?"

"I've already told the police." He stood up as if to challenge her and scowled at us. "I want to clear up my papers and be done with it."

"And what did you tell them?" I wasn't sure whether Sherlock or I asked that question.

Mr. Tessmeyer sighed. "She was a good psychiatrist, but you won't find many who liked her. I certainly didn't." He walked over to the door and opened it. Light streamed into the room. In the brightness, he didn't look as old as he had before—maybe a decade younger than me.

"Was Dr. Randall blackmailing you?" El said standing her ground.

His face turned bright red. At first, I thought the man might be having a stroke. He looked taller, with his shoulders thrown back like a belligerent bull.

"Do you know anyone else she might have blackmailed?" El wouldn't stop.

The question surprised Mr. Tessmeyer. "I'm not sure."

"If you do, it might be helpful to tell us." El stared at Mr. Tessmeyer, and he stared back. Sherlock and I could have been on a different planet. "But it might help you too." She put a hand on his arm. "Your mother is a wonderful lady. She shouldn't have to worry about you going to jail."

He rubbed his hands together. "I'm not proud of what I did, but I didn't break the law."

"The police will think that you had a good motive for killing her when they find out she was blackmailing you. Believe me, they will find out."

He took in a quick breath. "I couldn't kill anyone."

El wasn't done. She grabbed the lapels of his smoking jacket and pulled him to her. "The police don't know that."

Tessmeyer whispered, "An acquaintance of mine, an old classmate, recommended her." The fight had gone out of him after this petite woman manhandled him. "After she started blackmailing me, I wondered if there were others. She had plenty of opportunity to find out everyone's secrets. My classmate never admitted she'd been extorting money from him when I called. I couldn't bring myself to admit it either." Tessmeyer shrugged.

"What's his name?" I asked, wondering why Sherlock was quiet. I'd expected him to jump into the conversation at any moment.

"I'll get his information for you," Tessmeyer said and left the room.

"That was scary," I said. Her assumption that he'd been blackmailed amazed me.

The rigid lines melted into her pretty face. "I made a wild guess." She looked away and focused on the doorway where Mr. Tessmeyer had disappeared.

I wanted to say more, but our host, which was really stretching the term, reappeared. Mr. Tessmeyer looked relieved. Maybe he thought we would switch out attention to his old classmate.

He handed me a small piece of paper. "Please don't tell him that I gave you his name. I don't want him to know. He'll talk about me."

"We don't know what you told Dr. Randall and don't want to," El said.

"Believe me, even a hint of scandal, and he'll be ready to make up the rest." He gestured to the door. "This has been an exhausting day."

Poor Mr. Tessmeyer had been in a bad spot. I was amazed that the smiling lady in pink had been capable of causing so much distress. "You need to tell the police," I said.

"They've interviewed me and didn't ask. Why should I tell them now?" He took a handkerchief from the pocket of his navy jacket and wiped his head.

"They'll discover that she was blackmailing you even if we don't tell them." I felt sorry for the man.

He looked up, his eyes wide, mouth open. Rudy didn't look like a murderer.

My dear, not every murderer has an ugly scar or a bad demeanor. We are done here. He has told us what he can.

El frowned, and lines wrinkled her forehead.

Maybe I did know everything I needed to know about Mr. Tessmeyer. Blackmail and murder? Mucking around in other people's lives wasn't right. I wouldn't want anyone messing around in mine "Thanks for your time," I said and pushed through the storm door.

Miss El is anxious to solve this puzzle.

El wouldn't stop, even if I refused to continue to investigate the murder. She might get in trouble without me. I suppose becoming an amateur sleuth to keep her out of danger would have to do. Perhaps it would even be fun.

Not an amateur sleuth, a consulting detective, Sherlock said.

Chapter 8

El slid into the driver's seat of my car without saying a word. Sherlock had already changed our relationship.

In the past, she'd been a bit pushy at times. But she didn't usually lord it over me unless I needed an extra shove. At work, El had never needed the limelight, but she could be relentless if she thought a doctor representing a medical supplier at an FDA reviewvpanel had lied to us.

Today, Sherlock put her into the driver's seat, literally and figuratively. I tried not to act offended since from her perspective, I'd told her she could drive. Meanwhile my master sleuth receded for the time being.

"What do you make of them?" I asked. As the sun emerged from a tattered white cloud above, Rudy peeked around the sheer curtain in the front window.

"Mr. Tessmeyer wasn't what I expected," El replied, as she drove down the street to Wisconsin Avenue.

We kept driving up and down Wisconsin Avenue like the ancient migrating bison and elk who'd created the path before the first settlers arrived. What had we expected to find? Motive and opportunity? It was true, Mr. Tessmeyer had definitely done something worthy of blackmail. The question, however, was whether he would commit murder to cover it up. His mom made him look like an uptight kind of guy afraid of his own shadow. While he didn't strike me as capable of murder, I had a feeling the man had his own secrets he wished to hide from the world.

The sun shining down on us was a welcome change. In the Maryland and D.C. area, the weather could change quickly. We liked to tell newcomers that if they didn't like the weather, they should wait fifteen minutes. The violent storms that sometimes blew through the region didn't happen every day.

Neither did the murders of hypnotists.

I kept thinking about Mrs. Tessmeyer. "Did she try to throw us off track?"

El shrugged. We reached the parking lot at El's condo in minutes—the Beltway traffic had been light. "Come on in. I'll make us lunch."

Despite the fact that her kitchen looked like it was never used, El was a master of gourmet meals. "Don't go to any trouble," I said while simultaneously hoping she would make me one of her airy omelets. She could easily work at some fancy restaurant; she just needed a tall white hat and maybe grow five inches.

El laughed. "I won't make anything too complicated."

Her laugh made me feel better. After she donned a blue and white checked apron, she did make me a Denver omelet, and one of the cheesier varieties for herself. While I sat at the mahogany dining room table, munching on my crustless toast, I mentally ran through the information we'd gathered about the Tessmeyers.

El patted her mouth with a napkin. "Rudy, right?"

"Yep. I'm sure he told his mom that Dr. Randall blackmailed him. They're probably pretty tight."

My friend cut another piece of omelet with the side of her fork. A string of cheddar cheese escaped from the forkful of egg she raised to her mouth. She laughed and put the tip of her fork back on her plate twirling the cheese into a tidy package. "It's hard to imagine Mrs. Tessmeyer as a controlling type."

This statement made me wonder if El's mom had been a control freak. In my family, nobody worried much about anything. I'd only been fourteen when my parents died in a car crash, and with my older brother gone, my young aunt and uncle became my guardians.

"I'm curious about Rudy's dirty deed."

I was pretty curious myself. "Can't imagine we'll find out."

"Something to do with a woman?"

"Didn't see any evidence of a Mrs. Tessmeyer at his house. I wonder what happened to her. If there is no wife in the picture now, an affair would be no big deal. Something to do with his business would make sense. There's a thin line between good business practices and fraud."

She nodded; her mouth still full.

"But could he kill someone?" I said. Mrs. Tessmeyer made a point of saying he couldn't.

Perhaps that is precisely what she intended us to believe, Sherlock added.

Mrs. Tessmeyer could've easily connected our unexpected appearance with the murder she'd heard about on TV, or Rudy might have told her the police questioned him.

"There's also the younger Mr. Tessmeyer," El said. "He might be the missing piece to the puzzle."

"Let's talk to him."

"Or revisit his grandmother?" El took my plate and walked into the kitchen. "Would you like some coffee?"

"Sure." I wondered if I should ask sooner next time or if she'd be weird about it. El had this thing about drinking water with her meal, but I preferred coffee.

"What should we do?" She seemed more consumed with the case than I could justify. We weren't trained like the police, and we hadn't known the doctor very well.

I shook my head before focusing back on what we'd learned. "Another visit to Mrs. Tessmeyer. But we need a new angle." Sherlock had said that we would go back and tell her what we'd learned.

When El joined me with two cups of coffee, she slid the paper Mr. Tessmeyer gave her across the table.

"I'm not sure I'm ready to talk to him yet."

El nodded. "We're not going to like him if he's the kind of guy who sells out his friends. If Dr. Randall blackmailed him, then he's also a suspect."

We should talk to the other tenants around Dr. Randall's office, Sherlock broke in, organizing my thoughts. I wasn't convinced we should. I might be able to convince El to stop this nonsense before we got that far.

"Mrs. Tessmeyer did ask us to stop by and tell her how it all worked out. If we ask the detective what progress he's made, we could tell her. We should do that first. He might have all of this figured out." I took a gulp of coffee. I would have drunk a whole pot if El would've let me.

She didn't get the hint. "We'll go back to Dr. Randall's office building after Mrs. Tessmeyer," El said. "What are we going to ask her once we catch her with her guard down?"

I had no answer to that. I didn't want El verbally attacking little old ladies. Had Rudy told Mrs. Tessmeyer about the blackmail? Would she be willing to add to what her son had admitted?

"Tomorrow," El said. "You should go home. You're looking pale." She did look concerned. If I had been the type that liked to be coddled, she would have found some way to take care of me rather than push me out the door.

"Tomorrow afternoon. I have an appointment in the morning." I was ready for a quick exit. My body wasn't feeling so hot, even if I didn't want to smoke. And I felt guilty about not telling her about Sherlock.

El picked up my denim coat and looked at her cell phone. Her smile faded away. "I have an errand to run too."

I didn't ask her what she needed to do. I'd forgotten how tough she could be until our interview with Mr. Tessmeyer. I'd experienced her compassionate side for quite a while which must have made me forget her killer instinct that had been so effective at work.

Your friend is very determined. Is there something else going on?

El had no connection to Dr. Randall except for setting up my appointment. I'd been so flustered by Sherlock's existence after my session, I hadn't stopped to think why she wanted to investigate the murder.

Indeed. And by the way, you are wasting your time going to a psychiatrist. I am real.

In the best scenario, the psychiatrist would diagnose me with some complex condition and commit me. Sherlock's existence was proof that I wasn't mentally well. This doctor might be able to give me medication, and poof, Sherlock would be gone.

Day Five
Chapter 9

Dr. Hessman's office in Gaithersburg was situated well away from my regular haunts, not too close to my condo and not too close to the Federal offices in Rockville or Bethesda. I wanted to make sure that I wouldn't run into any of my old workmates or acquaintances. A Hungarian restaurant that Harry and I had liked, located in the same small shopping area as her office, made it easy to pick her out of the list of psychiatrists in the phone book. I hadn't been to the restaurant since Harry passed away.

There would be time enough to tell El about my appointment after they locked me up.

The pictures in the psychiatrist's office had no rat people. Actually, there weren't any people at all in the abstract blue and green paintings. I decided that might be a good sign.

A highly visible receptionist behind a small glass door, that she slid to the side, welcomed me when I signed in. The receptionist's smock matched the pale green walls behind her. The music in the background, minus running water and bird sounds, whispered a pointless melody.

Alone in the waiting room, I didn't have to make small talk with someone who might turn out to be a killer. Of course, I reminded myself, I shouldn't talk. I might find myself accused at some point.

Sherlock hadn't said a word this morning. I almost missed him. At a few minutes before eleven, the receptionist asked me to come back to Dr. Hessman's office. "Your appointment is over precisely at eleven fifty-five when the doctor tells you that your time is up. You'll leave by the back door of her office which takes you directly into the hallway. That's how we protect your privacy. You will most likely never meet any of the doctor's other patients." Her voice was barely louder than a whisper.

"How will I settle my bill if I don't see you after my session?" It was hard not to imitate her tone, kind of like how you start talking with a foreign accent after you've been abroad for a while.

"I'll charge your health insurance if I can. If not, the full amount will be charged to the credit card you gave me over the phone. You only need to talk to me if you need to make other arrangements to pay for your sessions. The doctor will make all of your appointments for you."

After the subdued tone of the waiting room, the bright sunshine streaming out of the of the office door, and Dr. Hessman, herself, surprised me. The good doctor was well over six foot, tall enough to play basketball if you counted the mass of blond curls on top of her head.

"Your receptionist's little speech lasted exactly as long as it took for us to walk down the hall," I said as I looked around the office. A regular couch, not a reclining one like I'd seen in the movies, took up one wall while a couple of lime-colored wingback chairs stood in front of the wide, bowed window that framed a courtyard. Outside, water still tumbled out of a fish's mouth from the fountain in the middle of the garden that had been cutback for the winter.

She followed my gaze to the window. "I suppose I'll have to turn off the spray soon, although we leave water in the pool all winter for the Koi. I love a living picture. You can't do something like that when you're on the tenth floor of a high rise. Would you like to sit down?" She sat in one of the green chairs, tucking her long legs neatly to the side and crossing her ankles.

"Thanks." The chair felt surprisingly firm as if too new to have developed a sag.

"Would you like to tell me why you're seeing me today?" Her mouth still smiled, but something had happened to her light-colored eyes, gray or maybe blue.

I paused and wondered if my visit had been a good idea. By the expression on her face, the doctor might not be ready for my story. But if I didn't tell her, then I'd wasted good money coming to see her. She would bill me even if my insurance paid a reasonable amount. And, after all, I'd come to see her so I could get rid of Sherlock. If I didn't tell her my problem, I didn't think I could get rid of him on my own.

"On Veterans Day, this other psychiatrist hypnotized me."

Her eyes widened, but she didn't interrupt. All of the other psychiatrists had probably been talking with each other about Dr. Randall's murder.

I told her about that day and how the police suspected El and my involvement.

"I don't see how I can help you. You should find a private detective."

I couldn't help myself. I snorted. Another detective was exactly what I *didn't* need.

For a second, she was so startled, I worried that I'd scared her away. Instead, she smiled. "That's quite a laugh you have."

My face warmed. "More like a snort of disgust."

"My suggestion disgusted you?"

I'd piqued her interest. "Do you want to hear more?"

My tall doctor didn't look so worried now. She nodded her head vigorously. I could turn out to be the most entertaining patient she'd had in a long time.

"In a way, I do have a private investigator." I paused again, studying her face.

"Go on." She pushed the sleeves of her black angora sweater up her muscular arms. A gold charm bracelet on her left arm jingled as she leaned forward, the color a deep yellow instead of a washed-out gleam. A heart, a stylized cat, a golf ball. More charms glimmered under the heavy gold chain.

"You see, I'm still in a trance."

"But you're talking to me now."

"Before I blacked out, I heard someone."

"You should tell the police." She wrote a note on her pad.

Perhaps she planned on calling the police herself. Suspected crimes might not fall under patient privilege or whatever they called it. "I didn't want to tell them because…"

"Because?" she prompted me. I needed to stop procrastinating.

"Because the voice was in my head."

The doctor's eyes widened. She wasn't smiling anymore. I was right that she must have heard about Dr. Randall's murder. "Did it tell you to do things?"

"Well, yes," I said softly, imitating her voice. I didn't know why I was still imitating her.

She stood for a moment, hand on her chair, before backing into the corner, knocking over a fantastic imitation Chinese vase about three feet high. It fell on the thick carpet. Almost in slow motion, the blue and white design marked by green leaves blurred and bounced into the leg of her chair. A crack sounded, and a piece of the vase, about the size of a small saucer landed at my feet.

"No," I shouted looking down at the vase, hoping it was an imitation. When I looked at her again, her pale eyes widened even more.

She squeaked out a strangled cry.

"No," I said again, this time in a normal voice. "It didn't tell me to kill her or anything like that." My drawn-out attempt to fess up about Sherlock had obviously misled her.

"You didn't kill her," she mumbled. She looked down at the vase realizing what she'd done. "Oh, no." She picked up the vase and put it back on the pedestal.

"You could glue it back together," I said sheepishly, handing her the piece in front of me.

The doctor glared at me and sat down in her chair, cradling the smaller pieces. "What did the voice tell you to do?"

"It told me," I started to say.

Sherlock interrupted. "For heaven's sake, I told her to open her eyes," he said taking control and jumping from the chair. "She believes she's insane. If you would just assure her that reincarnation does happen, we can put all this behind us and solve the case." He paced back and forth.

"And you are?" she asked cocking an eyebrow.

"I am Sherlock Holmes, of course," he said and stood with hands on my hips. I tried to break in, but he wouldn't let me. He was angry, extremely angry about me wanting him to go away.

Dr. Hessman froze for a moment before she started to laugh. I thought she'd gain control of herself. She didn't. Tears rolled down her face.

"Do you see?" he said aloud. "This doctor is not worthy of our patronage."

I quickly seized control. "I don't believe in reincarnation."

The doctor waved a hand at me and pointed to the door. "When I stop laughing," she gasped, "I'm going to be very angry at you for wasting my time, and I won't be going on a talk show with your ridiculous story."

I grabbed my coat and made for the door. "I'm not giving up," I said to Sherlock, not caring if the doctor heard me or not. "This life is mine, not yours."

He receded back to his Victorian chair by a roaring fire, puffing away.

No. No one, no matter how many of us there are, will ever be allowed to smoke again. The picture of him disappeared as quickly as it had popped into my head.

My track record with psychiatrists wasn't good. Dr. Randall had been killed, and Dr. Hessman had laughed me out of her office. I might be tempting fate if I tried again.

Yet the thought of having Sherlock in my head forever infuriated me. If he was a ghost, why couldn't I see him? That would be easier to take, although it might be enough to push me over the edge. None of that would matter, none of it at all, if the police locked me up for murdering my hypnotist.

Chapter 10

I arrived at El's place still angry—so angry that I'd forgotten to go to the restaurant that Harry and I had reserved for special occasions. And I was starving. The most El would offer me at this hour was a cup of coffee. She didn't even offer me that. Instead, she handed me Detective Kirkland's card even though I still had a copy tucked inside my purse.

I didn't want to talk to him. His cold gaze had not matched his melodious voice that had sounded so warm and comforting when I first met him. I suppose he could have been nervous too or simply a restless soul who cultivated a calm exterior. When I lit up often enough, smoking had calmed my nerves. I pushed that memory out of my mind as I pulled out my cell phone.

"Detective?" Silence greeted me from the other end of the line. Kirkland probably took one last puff before he threw his cigarette to the ground outside police headquarters.

"What can I do for you Ms. Holmes, or should I call you Mrs. Carpenter?"

Why had I suddenly switched back to my maiden name? I'd been putting the wheels in motion to change my name officially for months. Every time, the forms I needed to fill out reminded me what a pain it would be to change my driver's license, Social Security info, and contact all the people who would need my legal name. But procrastination wasn't the only reason I hadn't gone back to my maiden name. I knew it was because I didn't want to lose Harry for good.

Sherlock was quiet. I was surprised that he didn't offer some cutting remark or rant at me about how stupid I was. El stared at me, twirling her finger as if to tell me to get on with it.

"Have you made any progress on the case?"

"I would be happy to tell you all about it over coffee," he said.

"We would be happy to meet you." I watched El as I talked, but thought about Sherlock, too. He could figure out what the detective was doing. My live-in visitor liked to tell me all about other detectives.

"Why don't you come alone. You can tell Ms. Franklin about our conversation later."

If I'd been in a good mood, I might have been flattered that this somewhat younger man had asked me to go for coffee. As it was, he might be using another tactic. Divide and conquer or something like that. "Hold on," I said. I put the phone behind my back. "He wants to meet with me alone." I tried not to show her that I wanted to go without her.

One of El's eyebrows shot up. She shrugged.

"When?" I said interpreting her response as a yes.

"How about now? There's a Starbucks with outdoor tables on Connecticut, close to the Beltway."

He wanted to smoke. How would I react when he lit a cigarette? But anything would be better than thinking about Dr. Hessman.

"I can be there in half an hour." The words came out of my mouth before I asked El what she thought, even though she had indicated that she didn't care if I went alone. One look from her said that I had made a mistake. I didn't want to alienate my best friend. I couldn't imagine a day, any day, where I didn't talk to her. She didn't look happy.

"See you then," the detective said and hung up.

"I won't go."

"You have to," she slid back into her chair. "It won't look good if you don't. I'm disappointed is all." She frowned.

"I don't like it. He's probably going to trick me." But I did want to find out more about him, what he'd been doing. My denim coat was on the back of the couch. I could fling it on and be out of the door in a minute.

"You're dying to go. So go," she said. "If only we had a bugging device so that I could listen in on the conversation."

She'd read my mind. I smiled. "If I take my phone out of my pocket and leave it on my lap, you might be able to listen."

Her face brightened. "Let's try it out. While you're in route, I'm going to see if it's possible to buy a bug online."

Back in the car again, I smiled when I realized I'd forgotten all about how angry I'd been when I arrived. El always had a positive effect on me. If only I wasn't going crazy, then this investigating stuff would be fun. These last couple of days had rushed by.

My days normally started more slowly with coffee, email, coffee, and until recently, a smoke. It's not that I wanted to smoke—that urge was gone—but my brain still wanted me to follow my usual routine, and that included smoking. I looked at those nasty little sticks that still resided in my purse, yet I didn't feel compelled to smoke them. I felt better in motion.

After I pulled my car off the Washington Beltway and stopped at a red light, I took a tissue from the pack in my purse and blew my nose. My poor sinuses, filled with black crud—and probably my lungs too—just wanted to clean it all out. I'd seen enough pictures in the evidence files at work. I kept expecting the crud to show up in my tissue.

The light changed.

Somewhere on the right was the Starbucks he'd mentioned. I wasn't exactly sure how far inside the Beltway the coffee shop was. Commercial properties lined Connecticut Avenue for the first few blocks before the street became lined with brick residences. They grew to mini-mansions crowding the sidewalks closer to Washington, D.C.

Parking might be a problem. Most of the businesses had limited parking along the street that appeared to be dug through the hill. But when I saw the green and black Starbuck's sign not far from the Beltway, a parking space was only a few steps away. I pulled in beside a dark green Ford that looked like it might be his because of the bar of lights nestled inside the rear window. Kirkland waved from a wrought-iron table as I stepped out of the car. He tossed his burning cigarette down and ground it under foot. "That didn't take long."

"Traffic isn't that bad today." Traffic and weather were always good ways to start a conversation. When I sat down, the iron chilled me, but I was sure it would warm up soon enough. The news had said that the high temperature today would be in the low fifties, not bad if there was no wind. I looked down at the smashed cigarette. "You might want to make sure you throw that away before we leave," I said, cigarette protocol still fresh in my mind.

"Sorry, I shouldn't be smoking. I know you quit. But there aren't that many places or times when I can smoke."

He didn't have to remind me of how difficult it was to smoke since they'd passed all those laws about smoking in public buildings.

You seemed to have solved that problem, Sherlock whispered.

I'd been wondering when he would show up again. It would be helpful if he didn't interrupt. I got confused about who was saying what.

I will restrain myself.

Kirkland watched me. He slouched a little in his chair, hands resting on his thighs, until he reached forward to pick up his coffee in a Grande-sized cup. "Do you want coffee?"

"I'll get it," I said and went inside. The young man behind the counter—not too young to be out of school, but young enough to have a fresh face—fixed my Tall cup. The cinnamon rolls were tempting. Instead, I called El. "I'm getting my coffee."

"Slip your phone into your pocket. After you sit down, take it out if you can." El whispered. She didn't need to whisper while I was inside. Kirkland was still outside, but I didn't want to explain that to El in front of the clerk.

"It might not work. Time to go." I retrieved my coffee from the counter, leaving a dollar in the tip cup, and walked outside even though I had no idea what to say or ask Kirkland.

If he still considers you a suspect, he will probably sit up, lean forward as he assesses you. You were right when you decided that his eyes will tell you more than any other part of his body.

The coffee burned my hand through the collar the young blond man had put on my cup.

Did you notice the color of the young man's eyes? Sherlock asked.

Why did it matter? He wasn't important. I shifted the coffee cup to my left hand.

Certainly not. But you must pay more attention to the world around you. Not all details are important, but you can sort them out after you know whether you will need them, or not. For instance, the detective's black shoes are freshly polished, but his jacket is crumpled as if he's worn it more than once.

So, he has new shoes. I took the lid off my cup and blew on my coffee.

His shoes are not new. The front toe of his left shoe has a small bit of leather that has been torn loose. The scuff, however, is the color of the shoe as if black was liberally applied to cover the blemish.

Okay, his shoes aren't new. I looked up and saw Kirkland watching me. I blew on my coffee again and put the lid back on. I would deal with Sherlock later.

The detective smiled as I sat. He was a different person when he smiled, not some stereotype from the old movies I'd seen. I glanced at the naked ring finger on his left hand.

My seat wasn't as cool as I remembered. I looked down. He would probably notice my phone if I took it out of my pocket. I decided to pull it out at least for a little while and hold it under the table where it was partially visible through the wrought iron. I flipped the phone over so it faced my body.

Kirkland leaned forward. "What did you want to know?"

"We're naturally curious." I took a small exploratory sip. Too hot. When the sun came out from behind the clouds, the day could have been in early October instead of the middle of November. The seasons had been slightly off the last few years. The leaves had been taking longer to change color.

You must focus.

"Dr. Randall's files are interesting." He watched every move I made until a truck rattled and groaned down the lane going south toward D.C. and pulled his attention away from me. He took another sip from his coffee.

"Okay, I'll bite. Why are her files interesting?"

"You should know. You visited Mr. Tessmeyer. How did you know he was at Dr. Randall's office that morning?" His bushy eyebrows lowered.

"Jessica told us." As soon as I said the words, I realized I'd made a mistake. He squinted as if staring into a bright light, making his glance colder and more piercing. I wondered how Sherlock would describe the detective's eyes. My impression of Kirkland before had been completely off the mark. Either that, or this guy's attitude was different.

"I told you not to interfere." The look on his face didn't change.

"We're naturally interested." I didn't see any reason to say more. Just because we talked to the Tessmeyers didn't mean we were investigating the murder.

"You must realize that Mr. Tessmeyer might be the murderer," he said.

"Does that mean El and I are no longer suspects?" If that was true, then there wouldn't be any reason for us to continue investigating Dr. Randall's murder. Sherlock wasn't happy that I was considering dropping the case.

When the detective didn't answer, I spoke again. "Aren't you going to tell me anything?" He was annoying.

Why wouldn't he give me an update? Had they talked to anyone?

His face relaxed. "We had narrowed the field of suspects to her patients. Mr. Tessmeyer's fingerprints were in the office. But he volunteered that information when we interviewed him. I'm not sure who else we should suspect."

If they considered all of Dr. Randall's hypnotized patients as possible suspects, that response would make sense. Perhaps it's not wise to tell him about the blackmail, Sherlock said, *After all, there would be no reason for Mr. Tessmeyer to tell us. We determined that on our own.*

He had done that without my help or approval by reading Tessmeyer's personal papers.

Even if I had broken into his house, if Mr. Tessmeyer was guilty, I do not think you would object to my methods.

A person's privacy was more important to us these days. I had to be cautious. I still hadn't decided if anyone noticed when Sherlock spoke to me.

"What's wrong?" the detective said leaning forward as if my face *had* revealed my inner conversation.

I wondered if I squinted or frowned when Sherlock talked. If I convinced Sherlock to talk to me when I was standing in front of a mirror, I might be able to look more normal in public.

You might not have the same expression on your face during such an exercise.

If I told El about Sherlock, she could tell me.

Dense clouds covered the sun. I felt like I had an itch that I couldn't scratch. This meeting had accomplished nothing.

I want to drink our coffee, Sherlock said. It did smell good. I ignored the detective's question and took a sip. The brew was the perfect temperature now.

"Ms. Holmes?" The detective's voice was more insistent.

"Yes?" The coffee helped. I took another sip. The cloud passed and the sun's rays warmed my face again. "Are all of Dr. Randall's patients suspects?"

"Do you mind if I have a cigarette?"

I shook my head and grasped my coffee with both hands to warm them. The patients she'd been blackmailing should be at the top of the list of suspects. We had identified at least two of them: Tessmeyer and his old college acquaintance. The doctor had probably increased her odds of finding worthy material by requiring her victims to give her referrals to people they suspected of fraud or worse.

He lit the cigarette and took a long drag before he said, "We haven't found the gun."

No one had said anything about the gun before. My hand didn't move to my purse. I had no desire to smoke the cigarettes in the inner compartment. "Who had the appointment after me?"

He froze. "What do you mean?"

"Dr. Randall told us that she didn't want to keep the door open to the waiting room because the next patient might disturb us." I was sure I'd told him everything she said during my treatment. But he hadn't asked me what had been said before we went into the pink room.

"No one was scheduled for an appointment after you." His eyes narrowed, and he balanced his lit cigarette on the edge of the table.

"I'm not making it up. Dr. Randall sounded like she thought she had another patient."

He took out his notebook and flipped it open, looking at me again before he scribbled something on the page. "You don't appear to have a motive to kill Dr. Randall. Your friend, however, is close to another patient that we suspect is a blackmail victim. That gives her motive and opportunity." He picked up his cigarette and let the long ash drop to the ground. The smoke from his cigarette drifted away caught by a gust of wind that came out of nowhere and swept a few brown oak leaves from the patio.

El had known about Dr. Randall's blackmailing scheme?

"That doesn't mean a thing," I said and added some expletive-deletives under my breath as I slipped my phone back into my pocket.

"Maybe it does, and maybe it doesn't." He took another puff that lingered in the crisp air.

"I'll leave you to your break," I said and took a gulp of my coffee.

Kirkland stood up. "Are you going back to report our conversation to Ms. Franklin?"

"You wanted me to come by myself. I did that. But El will want to know what you told me. As far as I can tell, not much."

"I thought you should know about your friend. Don't make a mess of things." He threw his cigarette to the sidewalk and smashed it with his shoe, the one that had the little flap of leather.

"I suppose you're going to tell me not to leave town, or something dramatic like that." I tried not to be so pissed-off. He thought he was doing me a favor or maybe it was another one of the games like the one Sherlock talked about.

"We don't say that anymore. I can find you." He waited for my response.

I didn't think I could say anything not trimmed with expletive-deletives arranged like obnoxious vegetables around a Thanksgiving turkey.

"I'm not done with my investigation, Ms. Holmes," he said and walked away.

The sun disappeared behind a dense cloud, and the wind started to blow. The leaves that danced across the interlocking red bricks of the patio made dry scratching sounds. I suppose I should have been more cooperative.

I do not understand.

I threw the cup in a nearby can. What didn't he understand? He infuriated me, he and this detective. My temper had gotten me in trouble again. Not only had I turned Kirkland against me, I was still cursed with Sherlock.

I didn't want to think about El.

"Go away," I said to Sherlock and bent down to retrieve Kirkland's smashed cigarettes. I don't know if anyone heard me talking to my fractured self or not. At this point, I didn't care. I texted El that I would see her tomorrow afternoon before I walked to the waste can to dispose of the smelly butts.

She texted me back right away. "Not now?"

"Didn't tell me anything," I texted back slowing to a stop.

"OK," El responded. She had to know what was wrong if she'd been listening. Who did she know who was a blackmail victim?

Mrs. Tessmeyer might have been wrong. El could've killed someone if she had no choice. I started my car. That's why she'd wanted to investigate the murder. She either killed Dr. Randall, or she suspected her friend had murdered the doctor.

El had hounded me to go to the hypnotist to help someone else.

Anger swept through me. I could barely drive. Sherlock was silent about her betrayal. If I asked him, I would be giving into my own insanity. Maybe I subconsciously figured out her betrayal and created Sherlock out of desperation. I focused on the road so I wouldn't take anyone else to hell with me.

Day 6
Chapter 11

El pounded on my door. I'd been sitting in Harry's chair all morning thinking about what I'd learned yesterday. If I answered the door, I would have to talk to her. I wanted to be left alone so I could wallow in my misery.

"Open up, Sissy," El yelled from outside my condo. I certainly hadn't buzzed her in. She must have slipped in the building when another resident left.

Life was really crap when you couldn't even trust your best friend. Dr. Randall could have found out anything about me.

I made my way to the door and put my hand on the cool metal.

"I know you can hear me."

At some point, I would have talk to her if only to tell her where to go. I was sure I could come up with some colorful expletive-deletives.

"I'm sorry," she said.

My neighbors were probably going to make me come out of my hole if the racket continued much longer. At least she'd said she was sorry. Mad or not, I didn't want to lose my best friend. But I didn't know if I could get past this and trust her again.

El's voice was muffled. "Let me in."

When I opened the door, I saw her usual perfectly coifed black hair had been blown out of shape. One wing stuck out to the side, and tears wet her face.

I stepped to the side to let her into the entryway.

She took off her beige swing coat and hung it on a peg by the door before she walked into the living room. When she saw I wasn't moving, she stopped dead in her tracks. "I am so sorry."

I was sure I looked terrible in my fluffy blue robe and slippers. Finally, I closed the door and walked into the living room. Harry's chair waited for me. If Aunt Pet and Uncle Roger had been home, I would have gone to their place in Bowie. As it was, the fire I'd lit in my white fireplace was all I had to keep me company.

"Who?" I asked.

El understood. She sat down on my couch, glancing at the stacks of unopened mail on my black coffee table. "Marcus."

He was El's last boyfriend—if any of them *were* boyfriends. She never seemed to get that involved with them, but she'd fallen for Marcus, a stunning black man with curly, graying hair and a smoothly shaven face.

"I thought you broke it off with him." El told me they were through last spring. He wanted to take their relationship up to a new level, and she didn't.

"I broke up with him because of what he did."

"Why did you agree to help him now?" If she hadn't liked what he'd been doing before, I didn't understand why she'd become involved with him again.

"He called me about Dr. Randall."

Words erupted from my mouth. "You betrayed me for someone you didn't love."

"I thought I loved him."

"And that was enough," I said and didn't finish the sentence. "Get out."

"He was—he is in trouble. More than you can imagine." She might not love him now, but I knew that she had at least been infatuated with him last Spring.

I looked down at my lap, because I didn't want to look at her. There had been a time that I was sure I was going to lose her to Marcus.

"I'm in trouble too," she said without moving.

The silence was unbearable. I raised my head.

El pushed her black hair away from her face. "He didn't know if he'd told Dr. Randall about me under hypnosis. He told her what he'd done. Last month, he finally told me the whole story."

"Did you hear what Kirkland said yesterday?"

She nodded. "I heard. Leaving your phone on worked."

"Then you know you're a suspect."

I am curious about the circumstances, Sherlock interjected.

El did that thing with her fingers that she does when she's nervous, grouping her fingers together on each hand and touched the tips of her fingers, one hand to the other. Anyone who knew her well would have known she was worried, or her mind was in some distant place.

"Did he violate some law?" I asked, trying to jerk her back to reality.

"A bunch of them."

Marcus was a doctor at the National Institutes of Health. El had met him at one of the confabs we occasionally had to discuss issues that affected all the health-related Federal agencies. I'd been there too. After noting his good looks, I'd been drawn back into the conversation about the purpose of the meeting. He seemed absorbed in the discussion as well. But El had reported back to me the next day that he'd already called her.

They'd been taking trips to the Caribbean and various European countries. Much to my surprise, she'd cut him loose last Summer. One day they were hopping on planes to exotic places, and the next, he was no longer a part of her life.

One bureaucratic sin topped everything else in our business, profiting from insider information. If he'd made money off something he worked on, they would have caught him by now when he filed his financial disclosure reports.

Sherlock took over. "What did Marcus do?"

"He didn't do it on purpose."

Instead of admitting the truth, he might have trumped up the problem as an excuse to see her again. Her old boyfriends had come up with worse. One radiologist from North Carolina moved to Virginia to be near her and, later, after she wanted to break it off, said he'd murdered his wife. He wanted El to provide him with an alibi. She complied since he'd been in Washington at the time of his wife's death. That guy had been creepy.

Marcus was different. I had no doubt that she didn't tell anyone else, but she'd kept me amused with tales about their romance. Her visits to tropical climes and other travel stories kept me occupied for a long time. If El had been so inclined, she would have made a great romance writer.

"Just telling a friend about work wouldn't break the law. He would have to do it for money." I knew policy folks who'd slipped up, but none of them ever profited from their mistake.

"We thought he'd told a lobbyist from the AMA," she whispered.

Mentioning the American Medical Association wasn't a guarantee that the information had been used inappropriately even if you saw their richly paneled conference room in D.C. that looked like a million bucks.

"The lobbyist passed the information on to his political contacts." El put her head on her knees. "At least, that's what we assumed when we saw the stock go down before the FDA released their decision. Later, Marcus found out the AMA didn't employ the guy. He was only attending one of their functions."

The story was getting uglier and uglier. The lobbyists were known for trying to influence the career employees at the Federal Agencies.

"Why did you say the decision came from the FDA when Marcus works at NIH?" I was afraid that I already knew the answer.

"I accidentally told him about one of my projects." She lifted her head. To my knowledge, he wasn't close friends with anyone else from our old agency. I suppose she'd only been involved, because she hadn't reported Marcus. I didn't think she would agree to doing anything illegal. "Marcus has expensive tastes."

It all made sense. Even a doctor was subject to limitations on his income when he worked for the Federal Government. Since the information came from the FDA, no one would assume he'd leaked the information unless they knew about his relationship with El.

If the stock for the company involved had plunged or risen dramatically before the FDA announcement, everyone associated with the review process had probably been investigated. Our Department Office of Inspector General kept track of what policy analysts did after they retired too. A lucrative job after retirement would have been enough to make them suspicious if she'd gone that route.

"He profited in some way."

"I thought he must have a wealthy family to be able to pay for all of our trips." She started to cry again. "The trips were gifts from the lobbyist."

"Does anyone else know?" I'd never known anyone who got away with selling information, especially if the stock market had taken a hit. Of course, they wouldn't talk about their slip to anyone either.

She shook her head.

"Whatever happens, you should pay back your share of the trips." The whole thing could break her financially, but better that than losing her pension.

El nodded. "I'm so glad to get it off of my chest. The police know Dr. Randall blackmailed Marcus."

"Did he tell them that you two were an item?"

El winced. "I hate it when you talk like that. Makes me sound like a piece of meat. He said that the detective knew we had been involved."

Someone else must have told Kirkland that El was friends with Marcus. Or, he had found her name in Dr. Randall's file. "What did he get treatment for? The Marcus I remember is pretty trim."

"Let's just say he had a habit he wanted to control." I could tell she wasn't going to say more by the set of her mouth.

I realized then how dark the room was. I got up and opened the drapes. Sunlight streamed into the room. When I opened the door to the balcony, the air was pleasantly warm.

"Are you still mad at me?"

"Ask me tomorrow," I said and walked back to the entryway.

She followed me and grabbed her coat. "Why don't you come to my place bright and early?"

I didn't answer her. She needed my help. Whether I would be willing to give her that help, I wasn't sure.

Chapter 12

A friend of Aunt Pet's had been checking on their cats for the past week. When I finally did get out of Harry's chair again, a look at the calendar reminded me it was my turn to check in on the Himalayans. Aunt Pet and Uncle Roger's house in Bowie, east of Interstate 95 that linked D.C. to New York and beyond, was a fair drive from my condo in Silver Spring. I wished that they were at home and not away on another one of their adventures.

My aunt was my mom's little sister and not much older than me—only thirteen years separated us. She and Uncle Roger had taken me in when I was a teenager. Over the years, the difference in our ages meant less and less. As I drove back from checking on Hector and Achilles, I couldn't stop thinking about what El had done. I wanted to talk to Aunt Pet. She would help me sort everything out. I decided to give it a try when I could use my land phone line. She'd given me her international phone number.

"Sissy," Aunt Pet sounded pleased. She was the one who'd given me my nickname. My given name Margaret, never felt like my real name. At sixteen, I insisted everyone call me Sissy, and when I was eighteen, I had my name officially changed to my nickname. My parents wouldn't have cared—at least I didn't think they would. For some reason, I'd been named after a great aunt they didn't like.

"Aunt Pet," I said.

"You're calling me as a parent, not a friend."

When I needed help or comfort, I did always call her Aunt Pet. "How's your trip going?"

"What's wrong?" She liked getting to the point.

"If you're in a hurry, I can call back later. Where are you anyway?"

"London. We're just getting ready to go out to dinner." She didn't sound annoyed.

My anger boiled up inside of me despite my efforts to calm myself. "El set me up."

"What? El wouldn't do anything to you."

I gave her the general gist of what happened, saying only someone had blackmailed El's old boyfriend. (Sherlock would have to be the subject of a different conversation.) Aunt Pet didn't ask about what Marcus had done. Telling her did make me feel better. Before I'd met Harry, she'd been my closest friend.

"Well. She seems to care more about this Marcus than she let on." I heard some shuffling in the background. "Say hello, Roger," Aunt Pet said.

"Hello, Roger," my uncle said into the phone.

I snorted a good one even though it was an ancient joke.

"What's wrong, lovey?"

"I miss both of you," I said.

"We miss you too. You should come with us next time. We're going to Egypt."

I hadn't traveled since Harry passed away. It had been fun taking an occasional trip with them, giving my life a more exciting flavor. I felt guilty about being so selfish. When Harry was alive, he'd acted like he didn't want to travel. All the brochures under the bed in the spare bedroom proved to me that he'd only done that to let me have time alone with my aunt and uncle.

My life had been compartmentalized from one person to the next. Why hadn't I been able to focus on more than one person at a time? I did yearn for some time with Aunt Pet and Uncle Roger. Any trip would be better than here. And I'd never been to Egypt.

Aunt Pet demanded that he give the phone back to her. "There now, that's better. You need to calm down," she said.

"Easier said than done."

"You quit smoking, right?" Her voice changed into her stand-in-mother tone.

"Day six." With everything else that had been happening, I hadn't given it much thought.

"Sissy, I'm so proud of you. Now I know that El has been a disappointment, but no one is perfect." I couldn't help but remember her saying the same thing about Harry once.

"She lied to me. What if the hypnotist hadn't been killed? She could have tried to blackmail me too." Instead of calming down, I was getting angrier.

"Are you hiding any skeletons?"

I laughed studying the flames in the fireplace. For all of my disagreeable behavior, I'd never done anything that could get me in trouble at work.

"El wouldn't have let that happen. She's your best friend. Order Chinese and read a book." Aunt Pet never steered me wrong with her advice. "Are you still reading Rex Stout?"

My mom had been a big fan of Nero Wolf. "I forgot what a misogynist Archie was."

"Was he? I always thought he just liked to chase women." She seemed perfectly at home talking about the dating habits of a fictional character even though she should be leaving for dinner. I wondered if she would be so sympathetic when she found out about Sherlock.

"He might as well have been using a scale of one to ten. Most women would say that ranking women based on their looks is misogynistic. Why do I still like Archie?"

"Perhaps it's because he's the perfect Watson for Nero Wolf. Stout had to make him bigger than life you know, manlier by their standards to make up for Wolf and his orchids."

They sound like an interesting team.

I hadn't said a word to Aunt Pet about Sherlock. I would, eventually. She was still my safe harbor.

I believe she would be a sympathetic soul.

She was, but I didn't want to burden her with my resident consultant while she and Uncle Roger were off on an adventure. If I told her now, she might hop on a plane for home. Besides, Sherlock was a problem that I had to deal with on my own.

"Sissy, are you still there?" Aunt Pet sounded worried that her little game of making me think about something else hadn't worked.

"Have you ever noticed how many numbers are in the titles?" I'd been reading all of Stout's books again after I was invited to a Nero Wolf society. El hadn't wanted to go, so I'd gone by myself. The other members were all interesting people. But I still wanted El to go with me to the luncheons.

"I suppose they were going through a trend like all the titles we saw with the word Girl this or that, or are those the ones containing novellas?"

In the background, I heard Roger asking her why she'd made him wear a tuxedo if they weren't going to eat outside the hotel. He did look smart in a tuxedo. It wouldn't surprise me if she made sure they were invited to plenty of fancy-dress affairs just so she could see him in full regalia.

"What are you wearing?" I asked. She'd stayed trim as she aged and liked to do herself up grand, as Mom would have said.

"Do you remember the baby blue beaded gown I wore in New York?" she whispered excitedly. I did indeed. They'd taken me to a big dinner put on by the Importers Association. Aunt Pet had been stunning, even for a woman of seventy-five. The powder blue color had gone perfectly with her silver hair.

"What about the beads?" She'd complained about losing some from the dress.

"The lady at my cleaners, Esmerelda, found beads to match the ones on the dress. She's so clever. She can find anything on the Internet now."

"I'm sorry Sissy. We gotta go," Roger said, after taking over the phone, his voice firm.

I look forward to meeting your aunt and uncle in person.

Aunt Pet took back the phone. "Sissy, are you okay?"

"I'm fine." They made me feel grounded. Even though they'd been young, they'd provided me with a stable home. As I'd aged, I realized what a sacrifice it had been for them.

"Make up with El." Aunt Pet hadn't had any trouble making decisions for me when I was a teenager either. Back then, I would have blown up and done exactly the opposite of what she recommended. It had taken a while for both of us to find some middle ground.

"I think I already decided before I called."

"Sure, you did. You just wanted to bounce the whole thing off me."

"Don't go getting all sarcastic on me now."

Aunt Pet laughed. "See, you're fine."

"I am. Have a lovely dinner."

"Tell El hello from us. I can't wait to show you the presents I bought for both of you in Vienna." Aunt Pet had wonderful taste. Even though I frequently threw on the first t-shirt and jeans that I saw in my closet, I appreciated the beautiful clothes she gave me. I should upgrade my image. It was a shame to let all those clothes go to waste. Dominoes would have to fall though. I would have to lose some weight.

You should have *discussed the situation with me,* Sherlock said. *I do not understand the workings of your government, but indiscretions also occurred during my time.*

I was sure they did. Several Sir Arthur Conan Doyle stories had military and foreign relations secrets related to the government. Nothing so trivial as unprofessional behavior.

If Detective Kirkland discovers that neither this Marcus nor Miss El had any connection to Dr. Randall's murder, I believe he will also be discrete.

El was the only suspect with both motive and opportunity to commit the crime. Kirkland warned me not to trust her. Even if the evidence kept stacking up, I knew my best friend wouldn't have killed Dr. Randall.

Tomorrow I would show up at her door, bright and early. Crazy or not, if I used Sherlock to help me, I might be able to keep her out of jail.

I could decide how our friendship had changed later.

Day 7
Chapter 13

When I showed up at El's condo the next morning, the door was unlocked. She yelled at me from her bedroom to grab a cup of coffee, she'd be done cleaning soon. I needed to do some cleaning myself. I'd been avoiding that heap of mail on my cocktail table for weeks. Under normal circumstances, El would have thrown a fit when she saw it yesterday.

If Mom was still around, she would have complained too. When I was a kid, she used to tell me that I could grow corn in all the dust that blanketed my room. Midwesterners said stuff like that even if they'd never lived on a farm. El said hard work always set her mind right.

Cleaning was definitely not my thing.

El turned off the sweeper—a sign that more instructions would be forthcoming. A moment later, she yelled again, suggesting I find Dr. Welker's number online while she finished.

"Didn't we decide to talk to Mrs. Tessmeyer again?" I said from the kitchen, taking a sip of coffee.

When El pushed the sweeper into the living room, I snorted. She looked very domestic with a red cotton bandana wrapped around her head. She raised a hand to her scarf. "It helps keep my hair nice." She rolled the sweeper to her utility closet. As she closed the door, she hesitated.

"I know," I said. "I should clean my place."

She smiled. I suppose she was still worried about me being mad even though I was trying to act normal.

"Let's go see Mrs. Tessmeyer. It couldn't hurt. We can go to Dr. Randall's office building tomorrow."

"Why don't you see if Marcus can see us today?" I wanted to find out who had tempted him into breaking the rules.

El frowned. "He hasn't retired yet and should be at the office. Do we really need to talk to him?"

"Did he tell you who gave him the trips?" I wasn't going to let her off the hook as easily as that. "You need to find out who you'll have to pay for your share. If you don't, it might get back to the Agency. And if it does, you can prove you didn't profit from his actions."

El sat next to me on the couch, her dark eyes filled with tears. "I don't think I'll have enough cash."

"Marcus might have some idea about how much the trips were worth. If you pay the lobbyist back right away, it will look better than if you wait."

"My condo is paid off."

She must have been thinking about mortgaging it. There was no way that she could owe the entire value of her condo. The prices of both of our homes had taken a hit when property values went down. I didn't think they'd gone down that much, and I didn't have any idea how much money she had.

"Why don't we find out how much we're talking about first."

"He probably isn't at work yet." She went to get her phone. I expected her to come back to the living room to make the call. Instead, she went into her bedroom and closed the door.

She needs to tell him that you know about the bribes.

I hadn't been thinking of the trips as bribes even though I'd told El she would have to pay back her share. The gifts were a conflict of interest. Marcus had taken advantage of their pillow talk. The gentlemanly thing for him to do would be to pay back the whole amount. Since he was taking the trips, he probably couldn't afford to pay for her share too.

El returned, wiping tears from her face. "I told him we needed to talk."

"And?" I prompted her. I hoped she'd feel better if she started thinking about the logistics of getting out of this mess.

"He wasn't crazy about the idea, but said we could meet him for lunch." She looked down at her jeans and Orioles t-shirt. "I better change."

Under Aunt Pet's influence, I'd chosen a red blouse with embroidered black seagulls and a black sweater to go with my jeans. My tennis shoes had stayed in my closet. With my nice black ankle boots, I looked respectable for once. "Where are we meeting him?"

"Panera Bread," El said, taking the scarf off her head.

"I hope he told you which one." I knew of at least three Panera Bread's close to home.

"The one on Wisconsin Avenue."

Of course, it would be on Wisconsin Avenue. That Panera was close to the Beltway. But I couldn't help thinking we weren't much better off than the animals that had followed the beaten path that had turned into Wisconsin Avenue. "Let's go," I said. If we left right away, we might miss the human herd at lunch time. A cup of soup, half an avocado and turkey sandwich sounded good to me. I should have asked Dr. Randall to make me more patient too.

"I'll be ready in about fifteen minutes."

Miss El seems to have accepted our interference in her affairs.

That was true and not typical for her. She was probably trying to make up for keeping me in the dark. If she'd told me about Marcus' problem, I would have helped.

Are you sure?

Maybe I wouldn't have helped. I never liked Marcus; he looked too perfect. Or maybe I hadn't liked him because he'd taken up so much of El's time.

El was ready in ten minutes, and looked perfect too in her simple khaki pants, beige sweater, and white, oxford shirt. I drove us over to Wisconsin Avenue and pulled into the lot behind the Market. As we walked to the corner building, only one person was waiting at the counter.

"Come on," I said, walking swiftly inside.

Half a dozen people were already behind us when we finished our orders. Multiple lines, one from each of the three registers, stretched to the door by the time we had our food. We worked our way through the crowd to a round table near the front where Marcus would be able to spot us when he walked in the door.

"Did you tell him you wanted to pay back the money?" I said after I'd finished my lunch.

El patted her mouth with her brown napkin. "I told him I wanted to protect myself. That we needed to talk." She frowned. "I hope he doesn't think I'm throwing him to the wolves."

"He should know better."

She had gone out of her way to help him, even taking the chance of going to Dr. Randall's office. Mrs. Tessmeyer was right. El would never harm anyone. And she knew me well enough to know I had no secrets I'd pay anyone to keep.

Do not blame yourself for doubting her. We cannot predict what even the most respectable person will do when placed in jeopardy.

That was all well and good, but I didn't think that El would have doubted me.

"When I told him that I wanted to pay back my share of the trips, he was angry and said something about how he wasn't going to give back the money he'd paid to the blackmailer."

"Did he tell you who gave him the trips?"

"A lawyer who works at one of those big firms in D.C."

"I don't suppose he gave you any idea how much money we might be talking about?"

"He didn't have any idea." El stared out the window. "He's late."

He was. We'd sat down at our table at eleven-fifteen. He'd said he would meet us at eleven-thirty. My watch said a quarter to twelve. The sun found a clear path to the window where we sat.

"I'm going to call him." She had her phone out and was going through her contacts before she'd finished talking.

If I was Marcus, I wouldn't be anxious even though I'd never been that impressed by him. Still, the sooner we coordinated our efforts, the safer he would be too.

"Marcus—" Her eyes widened as she handed me her phone. "He wants to talk to you."

Why would Marcus want to talk to you?

"Hello?"

"It's me," a melodious voice said. It was Detective Kirkland.

"Why do you have Marcus' phone?" I was afraid to hear the answer after I remembered the gun used to kill Dr. Randall was still missing.

"Dr. Samuel is dead."

"Did he kill himself?" Next to me, El's eyes widened, and I wondered how she would react. It wasn't hard to imagine

113

him panicking and using the gun that he'd used to kill Dr. Randall. As horrible as it would be for El and, of course, Marcus, it would put an end to this drama. With the murder solved, Detective Kirkland would be out of the picture, and El and I could find the lobbyist who'd started it all.

"He didn't shoot himself," Kirkland said. "Where have you been?"

"We've been having lunch at Panera on Wisconsin Avenue. Marcus was supposed to meet us here at eleven-thirty." I looked over at El who was openly weeping now. One of the employees was at her side with a stack of napkins. My watch said it was now twelve.

"It happened about an hour ago." There was a pause on his end of the line. "How long have you been with Ms. Franklin?"

"I arrived at her place a few minutes after ten."

El pushed the Panera lady away and stared at me. We were an island of misery among the happy customers chattering away.

"We'll have to talk to the people there to verify your story."

"You can't be serious. She's been with me the whole time." Only last night, I'd talked about El being suspicious and today, I resented Kirkland for suspecting her.

He has to eliminate her as a suspect.

"Where was Marcus when it happened?" The best idea I'd had today was to take this conversation outside. If the

114

people around us heard me, it would cause a ruckus. I wish that we'd called Marcus sooner.

"He was in his parking garage," Kirkland said, more cooperative than he'd been before. He seemed convinced that whoever killed Dr. Randall had also killed Marcus. If that was true, we shouldn't be suspects anymore.

"There must be security cameras." We depended on the cameras as a deterrent at my condo building, and we hadn't had any muggings since they'd upgraded the security system.

"If the perp hadn't sprayed paint on the lens, we might have a better idea who shot him. As it is, we only have an eyewitness who saw a person in gray sweatpants and hoodie walk into the garage. They didn't see a face."

"I see." The sound of a car coming up behind us on the side street made me turn.

"Wait for me where you are," Kirkland said.

"I'm taking El to my car in the market's parking lot, the one in back. See you there."

In the bright sunshine, a white-haired woman walked across the red brick sidewalk that wound its way through a decorative hollow in front of Panera. She looked at us a little too long when she paused and leaned on her red metallic cane. There were three kids, two boys who might be around eight and ten, and a small blond girl who was much younger—about three years old—coming out of the front door with a tall man struggling to make them behave. They were halfway down the ramp before stopping in their tracks. The little girl pointed in our direction.

Was someone else watching us? Not the old lady or the children, someone who hadn't given themselves away. I don't know why the person who killed Marcus would have a reason to kill El unless they thought she might identify them. I walked faster, practically jogging over to the parking lot.

I unlocked the passenger door. The wind rattled the dry leaves still in the trees behind us. "Get in."

"Outside suits me better than waiting in the car. That detective did tell you to wait for him here, didn't he?"

On the west side of the parking lot, a red car with a squared off trunk like an old Mustang stopped at the end of the row of cars leading to the exit. There were plenty of parking spots closer to Panera. Over half the lot was empty. Yet the car was blocking our escape. I still had El's phone in my hand. I called Kirkland back.

"I'm getting creeped out."

El stared at the car which had peeled out and was headed in our direction.

"Get in the car," I yelled.

El got in and closed the door.

Kirkland was yelling at me. "What's going on?"

The car sped by and squealed around the turn to the exit where the truck blocking the street had finally moved. All I saw was a hooded figure through the smoky glass.

"I'll be there in five minutes. Don't do anything. Stay in the car."

I slid in and locked the door. "This is silly."

El tapped my arm. "Hang up. End the call."

I'd forgotten that Kirkland was still on the line. I handed her the phone.

"Marcus was always getting under people's skin. He had a way of irritating people," I was surprised to hear El say. Being irritable had always been my role.

"You don't get shot just because you irritate people." If everyone I irritated took a shot at me, I'd have been dead long ago.

Kirkland appeared in the parking lot across the street fifteen minutes later, pulling up beside us and rolling down his car window.

El's eyes were wide. "They drove past us after we were in the car."

"Some kid in a hoodie. My imagination got the best of me," I said.

Kirkland stared at us for a moment. "What were you doing here?"

El forgot who he was and told him. "Sissy wanted to talk to him."

I felt the pressure building inside Kirkland. All of the people getting in and out of their cars blurred as I waited for the explosion.

"I should lock you up." His voice was so loud, a couple getting into a black Ford truck looked to see what was going on.

"Can you at least keep it down?" I said instantly regretting my response. I always seemed to say the wrong thing.

On occasion, when people are upset, they do require a gentler touch.

Being advised on human relationships by a fictional character only lit that nasty short fuse of mine. Expletive-deletive-deletive.

Kirkland took a deep breath. I waited for him to exhale while I counted to ten and, somehow, my own anger dissipated.

"You're not supposed to be doing this." An understatement. I'd been surprised when he'd given me that much information on the phone. He'd been acting like we were investigating the case together.

"I totally agree with you detective," El said much to my surprise. With Marcus dead, her part in this affair was over after she paid some restitution to the D.C. lobbyist. What a skunky creature this lobbyist must be. I hadn't said anything to El, but I suspected that he might not take whatever money she offered him. That might be construed as an admission of guilt on his part. "Let's go, Sissy."

"I haven't told you that you can go." Kirkland's face was still red even though his voice had gone back to an even keel, soft and melodious.

"You should do something about that temper of yours," I said. I didn't mean to goad him, but I felt like he'd been bullying me since I'd met him.

"I am getting help. What's your excuse?"

"We don't want to keep you any longer than is necessary. I'm sure you're anxious to get back to Marcus' garage." El's voice was steady as if she was totally in control. By the end, her eyes filled with tears again.

If only I hadn't jumped to the conclusion that whoever killed Marcus might try to kill her. I've been wasting time.

What a strange saying. Time is a constant. You're not wasting time as you so eloquently put it. Detective Kirkland's actions seem to indicate that he was also worried.

"Is El in danger?" I asked.

The wind had picked up since we got out of the car. Fragments of brown leaves were twirling like a dust devil not far away.

"I don't know," he said rubbing the side of his face. "She should be very careful for the next couple of days." He studied my face. "Both of you. Can she stay with you?"

My place was a mess. The mail on my coffee table wasn't the only pile of stuff around my house. A pile of old magazines had slid across the floor by Harry's chair. Oh crap, I would have to clean my condo. At least I'd done the dishes.

"Is that okay?" El said watching my face.

"Of course," I said and wished I would stop saying of course. I was dithering.

"I'll leave after I get a statement from the employees here. You don't have to wait." Kirkland surveyed the small parking lot. "I'm not surprised you started freaking out. Anybody with a rifle would have had a clean shot at you from a dozen places."

"I was being ridiculous." The killer might not have even had enough time to make it here from Rockville. In fact, I was sure that there hadn't been enough time for the killer to make it to Panera unless they arrived after El and I were in the parking lot.

"You might want to remember," he paused, "both Dr. Randall and your friend Marcus were killed with a hand gun."

"Not a rifle," I finished for him. I didn't know if I would prefer worrying about the pedestrians we encountered or some invisible sniper in the tall buildings surrounding us. The car was too hot after sitting in the bright sunshine for so long.

If I could keep anyone, especially someone in a hoodie, from getting close to El, she should be safe. It was time to go home.

Chapter 14

"You're going in the wrong direction," El said as we left the parking lot.

"I'm taking you back to my condo. We can watch one of your talk shows and eat in tonight. I have steaks in the freezer."

My imagination was in full swing once again. What if we found ourselves face-to-face with the killer in an aisle of the supermarket? The delivery guy for my Chinese food always wore a hoodie too. The killer could always take him out, kill the delivery guy, and make short work of us. Protecting El might not be as easy as I'd assumed.

"Nobody's going to shoot me." She lowered the visor and smoothed her hair.

"Your hair still looks good," I said. Even now she was obsessed with how her hair looked.

"We're going to visit Mrs. Tessmeyer," El responded as if I would automatically do what she commanded.

Maybe last week, I would have. Today, I needed to be the sensible one. "Detective Kirkland suggested we go back to my condo." I glanced her way. Her mouth opened before I cut her off. "Not this time."

"What do you mean not this time? You and your detective are both nuts. I'm not stopping now. We need to talk to Mrs. Tessmeyer as we promised."

I agree with Miss El. The culprit will already know that if she could identify the murderer, she would have told the detective when he was here.

"You're no longer a suspect," I reminded her, ignoring Sherlock. "There's nothing you can do for Marcus now." It was a cruel way to end the conversation, even though Marcus was someone we had both known. No one deserved to die as the victim of a violent crime. The culprit, as Sherlock called him, *had* gone too far.

"Are you sure Marcus didn't tell you anything? Maybe some small thing that would point us to the murderer? What did he say when you called him?"

"He seemed disappointed I wasn't backing off. I think he understood that I had to pay back the money he'd spent on me or he wouldn't have agreed to meet us." She buried her face in her hands.

Sherlock gave me a mental pinch, insisting we turn around. Time was running out. The shooter might have a list of people to eliminate. I pulled into the left lane to do a U-turn.

El looked up. "What are we going to tell Mrs. Tessmeyer?" she asked as if she knew I would do the right thing.

"Let me think."

If we lay out all the facts before her, perhaps she can help us figure out what to do next.

I was sure my live-in detective had already decided what he'd do.

I have. We need to talk through all the facts and collect more information. It is possible that she will try to mislead us. If so, that will be worth knowing.

He made it sound so easy. The more information we gathered, the more impossible a solution seemed to me. The murderer might be watching us right now.

We found an empty parking space a block away. People casually strolled up and down the sidewalk. Looking for someone in a hoodie, I moved my head back and forth so many times, it made me dizzy. A person bumped into El close to the door of Mrs. Tessmeyer's building. The guy (hoodie-less) could have taken a shot right there. I panicked, pushing her inside.

"You're scaring me," El said, catching her breath.

"I would never forgive myself if anything happened to you." No matter what crazy thing she'd done, I *would* always forgive her.

"Nothing is going to happen with you around." She gave me a brief, but tight hug.

A shadow covered most of the entryway as the sun sunk to the horizon, too dark for me to be comfortable under the circumstances. If the killer decided to catch her here, we would be trapped. I watched her talk on the intercom to Mrs. Tessmeyer, wishing we could go up right away.

Yesterday, you were never going to speak to her again, Sherlock reminded me.

I shrugged mentally as the door buzzed. "Let's go."

When the door closed behind us with a click, I peeked through the semi-opaque sheers on the French doors. No one had followed us.

If the killer is outside, all they have to do is wait.

I wished Sherlock didn't pipe up like that. The elevator made me feel trapped, and the narrow hallway upstairs wasn't much better. At a door next to our destination, an ancient lady with a cloud of white hair cracked her door to peek at us without undoing the chain. I smiled and did a little wave before she slammed her door. Relief flooded through me when Mrs. Tessmeyer appeared and ushered us inside her home. It seemed like she'd been waiting.

"Another person has been murdered?"

"Another blackmail victim." I sipped the black tea that she'd recently prepared almost as if she knew when we would arrive. The cookies dipped in chocolate rested on a pretty plate painted with pink roses and light green leaves.

"We need to call Rudy," El said. "If the killer is going after blackmail victims, he could be in danger too."

We didn't need to tell Mrs. Tessmeyer twice. She pulled a cell phone from the pocket of her black cardigan. I had half-expected her to toddle into another room to a land line.

After her call, she eased herself out of her chair. "We'll need another cup."

I would like to talk to Mr. Tessmeyer again.

He always wanted to talk to people.

"I'm curious," El said, "why that detective changed his mind. We were all murder suspects and now the blackmail victims are the targets."

When Mrs. Tessmeyer returned, she suggested they wait for Rudy. "He only lives five minutes away." She leaned forward from where she'd settled in her chair and took one of the plain cookies from the plate, wincing before she adjusted the pillow behind her back.

It was no surprise when Sherlock took over. We walked to the corner bookcase by the window. "A blackmail victim would have a built-in reason to kill Dr. Randall. Whereas, not all of her patients would be obsessed with her." He pointed at the object before us. "Can you tell me about this pot? The one with the copper glaze."

"A friend of mine bought it for me at an estate sale of a mutual friend. I don't think it's English as she assumed. It doesn't bear a mark."

"I remember seeing such pieces before. The glaze is very distinctive."

"English?" she asked.

"Yes, but if I remember correctly, they did bear a mark. Early eighteen hundreds?" Sherlock was interested in the most mundane subjects sometimes.

Mrs. Tessmeyer rose from her chair and joined us by the curio cabinet. "Early twentieth century, if it's American. Perhaps 1910?" She opened the cabinet and handed the five-inch pitcher to Sherlock. She probably owed her amateur antique expertise to *Antiques Roadshow*. Everyone who watched PBS programs were exposed to at least little snippets about rare finds or the junk mistaken for treasures. They frequently used clips of the shows to fill the gaps between other programs. Sherlock placed the pitcher back in the curio cabinet.

The front door opened, and Rudy rushed into the room.

"Mr. Tessmeyer," El said, rising from her seat. That was a strange twist from the way she'd talked to him before.

"Another death?" he said as he tossed a leather overnight bag by the archway to a chair on his left. The alcove held a large dark table with six chairs carved in a fancy style. I'm sure Mrs. Tessmeyer would've run to him if she had been able. Instead, her son crossed the distance between them and gave her a hug before helping her back to her chair.

We quickly brought him up to date about Marcus.

"I'm sorry about your friend. He was killed with a handgun too, you say?" He put a hand to his forehead. "I don't have a gun, thank goodness."

Anyone could get a gun nowadays. Go into one of the neighborhood bars in D.C. and if you sat there long enough, someone who might sell you a gun would most likely appear.

At least, that's what I'd heard on one of the exposes about D.C. crime. I'd never tried to buy one myself.

"Did Detective Kirkland ever talk about the gun?" El said.

The afternoon sun angled in through the corner windows across the floor. Mrs. Tessmeyer's cozy condo seemed safe surrounded by her treasures.

El was trying to gain control of her shaking hands, dropping the sugar cube she was trying to put into a flowered cup with a set of silver tongs. A tear ran down her cheek.

"All I remember is that he told me that Marcus was shot with a handgun, just like Dr. Randall." He hadn't mentioned anything else.

"What about the missing keys?" El asked, brushing the tear away.

"I should have asked when I saw him." My hand took the tongs from El and dropped the sugar cube into Rudy's cup. When I tried to pour myself another cup, only a few tablespoons came out. Mrs. Tessmeyer took the empty pot from me and went to boil more water.

"What keys?" Rudy piped up from the entryway where he was hanging up his coat.

"The keys to Dr. Randall's files."

Rudy faced his mother when she returned. "The killer probably has my file."

"Now, we don't know any such thing."

Mrs. Tessmeyer must know that Dr. Randall had blackmailed her son. I wondered if El wanted to question Rudy again. If he was going to tell us everything we wanted to know, she wouldn't need to say a word.

The kettle whistled a high-pitched scream in the kitchen prompting Mrs. Tessmeyer to return to the kitchen. We waited until she returned.

Sherlock took command once more. "Detective Kirkland told me that the blackmail victims were suspects. I'm sure Mr. Randall is also on his list because he is Dr. Randall's husband. Wife-killing has always been popular."

El looked at me sharply as Mrs. Tessmeyer put the teapot back on the tray. Sherlock's last statement was as blunt as she'd been earlier. I guess Sherlock and El had changed roles.

Rudy's face lit up. "Detective Kirkland considered another possibility."

"If someone discovered that Dr. Randall made considerable sums by blackmailing her patients," Mrs. Tessmeyer frowned, "they might decide to take over her business?"

"That would explain why the keys are missing," El said.

"We'll know soon," Rudy said, lowering his head. I wondered how much money he'd already lost.

"Now that Dr. Randall is gone, the blackmailer might have contacted Marcus again, afraid that he would tell us who was demanding money from him."

Perhaps her husband will make restitution. Although such money is frequently squandered.

If they had managed their money to begin with, they wouldn't have to resort to blackmail.

Indeed, Sherlock affirmed.

"No one else has demanded any more money from you?" El asked.

Rudy shook his head. "Did someone contact your friend?"

"He said we would talk at lunch. I never had a chance to ask him if someone referred him to Dr. Randall like your friend."

"As I told you before, the term friend isn't quite accurate."

"He might have thought Dr. Randall could help you." El had the decency to blush.

"Have you spoken to Williamson?" Rudy asked her. "If you have, his character—or lack thereof—was probably obvious to you. She must have had plenty of dirt on him. The doctor was very skillful at pulling out deep and dark secrets. Personally, I hadn't thought about my indiscretion in years." The room went still.

Such creatures are willing to sacrifice others to save themselves.

Williamson hadn't sounded pleasant at first, but he sounded even more dangerous now. The sleazy side of Washington probably suited him.

"We haven't talked to Dr. Randall's other acquaintances."

"The people who work in the offices on the same floor might have seen strange goings on," Mrs. Tessmeyer said. Her sharp black eyes caught mine.

I hoped she hadn't noticed when Sherlock talked. I'd done most of the talking today while he confined himself to making comments only to me. I was getting better at not mixing up my conversations with real people with my conversations with him.

I decided once again not to tell El about Sherlock. She wouldn't believe in reincarnation any more than I did. Lately, I was starting to think that I was haunted by an ancestor of mine, perhaps thinking themselves to be the great detective.

I resolved to tell El about Sherlock once this business was done, and we were safe once again.

Day 8
Chapter 15

"I'm not sure it's a good idea to go out today," I mumbled. Last night, we'd argued about the possibility of the killer targeting her. I couldn't forget how afraid I was that someone might shoot El.

She had spent the night in my spare room after helping me clear off the bed. It hadn't taken us long once she found several black garbage bags. I hadn't been able to bring myself to throw away Harry's papers after he died even though I didn't want them. He'd saved crossword puzzles out of newspapers for years and collected books of them without completing them all.

"I'm not going to sit around all day." El snapped me out of my thoughts. She'd washed her shirt and pants last night so they would be clean for today. Her white shirt and khaki pants were wrinkle free thanks to the iron she found in the guest bedroom—it'd been a couple of years since I'd used the iron. "I'm not a blackmail victim," she said. "And Marcus didn't have a chance to tell me anything." She obviously wasn't worried about the possible threat to her life.

"The killer doesn't know that," I said, watching her face.

Exactly. We must protect her even if she does not have knowledge that would help identify the culprit.

If the killer had been watching her, they would know that she talked to Kirkland after Marcus' murder. But there were other logistics to consider.

I agree. You were right to wonder if the killer was able to travel from Marcus' home to the Panera restaurant in the allotted time.

El's lips jammed tightly together; she looked like she might explode. "Like I said, I'm not going to sit around your condo all day. You can keep watch all you want."

I couldn't protect her out in the world.

She waited for me to say something, and sighed when I didn't agree with her. There was no point in arguing so I kept silent. "I'll take that to mean you agree."

"Should we make an appointment with Welker?" I asked.

"Not unless you want to pay whatever he might charge by the hour."

His charges were probably too high. "Let's drop in and see what happens."

The gray sky looked like snow when we parked across from Dr. Randall's office building. El fed our parking meter while I kept watch since the Bethesda parking police made a tidy living from the meters. I'd seen a meter maid waiting for a meter to expire more than once. The lack of pedestrians on the block made me more suspicious. I felt like I was watching one of those black and white movies where the actors are waiting for the staggering zombies to appear.

We'd found Dr. Julius Welker in the online Yellow Pages, listed on Wisconsin Avenue. He didn't use the same Middleton Lane address as Dr. Randall which I thought was strange. El didn't think it was important. She said he probably thought it would be easier for prospective patients to find him on Wisconsin Avenue.

I hadn't been familiar with Middleton Lane before. Everyone who worked for the Federal Government—or lived close to Washington—knew Wisconsin Avenue because of the National Institutes of Health and the hospital located there.

Inside, only one person sat in Dr. Welker's waiting area—his receptionist.

"Dr. Welker might be able to see you. Did you want to have a session with him?" She wasn't exactly rude, just to the point.

I could imagine the wheels turning in El's head. Would she tell him about me asking who people were when I woke up from the trance? I decided to speak up before she fabricated a wild story about me.

"My friend here," I pointed at El, "has been going to Dr. Randall. Of course, with recent events…"

The look on El's face was priceless. She'd been trying to come up with a story about me. If she'd only thought about telling the truth, that I wanted to quit smoking, I would have kept my peace.

Her lips formed a tight line. Before today, I'd only seen her mad once in all the time I'd known her. Some wisecracking doctor on a government panel pinched her as she walked past him. The audience had seen her reaction to him even if they hadn't noticed the initial trespass. When she heard the group of Federal employees and attendees suddenly go quiet, she'd regained control—lucky for the offender. Needless to say, he was never invited to participate in one of our panels again.

Dr. Welker's receptionist's eyes widened. "I heard they read all of her files. But you mustn't be embarrassed," she said to El. The hard lines carved into her face didn't disappear.

I truly would have liked to know what was hidden away in El's mental closet. When I tried to imagine any secrets she might have, nothing came to mind aside from the trips she'd taken with Marcus.

"I would prefer to speak to the doctor," she said. As usual, she had the perfect answer.

The receptionist nodded, intrigued. "We *are* very careful about our patients' privacy. In fact, his notes are all on his own personal computer, not accessible to anyone but himself."

"Do you suppose I could talk to him before I decide if I would like to book an appointment?"

"His time is very valuable."

I imagined she didn't want to look directly at El since they were obviously not busy. The receptionist almost looked like a real nurse in her crisp white uniform, with some sort of pin on her pocket. When I took a closer look at her name tag, it did say Dorothy Barker with an R.N. after her name. The doctor paid a registered nurse to keep away unwanted visitors. The interview techniques for doctors that I'd learned at work weren't going to help me with his watchdog. But if I prompted her, she might want to talk about recent events.

"Nurse Barker." I waited as she switched her frowning gaze to me. "Perhaps you could make an exception for my friend. She brought me along today because, well, after what happened with Dr. Randall, she wants my opinion."

That seemed to make our nurse pause for a moment. "So terrible, the murder and all. We didn't approve of her methods, so commercial."

"I was disappointed that one of my other friends referred me," El said pointedly to me. The switch of guilt from herself to another friend (really me) was seamless.

"Well, no one will be referring any more patients to her." The nurse then picked up her phone and pushed a button before she whispered something.

A look around the office gave me the feeling that Dr. Welker's practice might have suffered from the competition with the dead hypnotist. The beige chairs were a little worse for wear. The pictures on the walls were cheap-looking prints, not like the expensive-looking rat pictures in Dr. Randall's office.

An older man in a white coat appeared. Ms. Barker whispered to him and he looked at us, smiling, before gesturing to El. "Come on back."

I followed her without asking if it was okay.

Dr. Welker looked a lot like his outer office—a little worse for wear. He was a tall, thin man with a bad comb-over of dark gray hair that looked more like a style a cartoonist might draw. Yet his personal office appeared to be newly refurbished with fresh, springy carpet and pristine furniture.

Dorothy stood behind us for a moment before discreetly closing the door.

The doctor was looking at me. "What did you want to ask me?"

Why did he think I was the prospective patient? My mind buzzed anxiously. I hoped the panic wasn't showing on my face.

"My psychiatrist was Dr. Randall," El blurted out

"Ah, yes, such a tragedy."

Neither he, nor El spoke further. I realized the doctor wasn't going to volunteer any information without us volunteering our own.

I decided to bite the bullet. "Were you in the office that day?"

"You're not here about an appointment," he said and put down his pen.

"We're trying to figure out what happened, is all," El said blushing, her tone apologetic.

"And you've put me on the list of suspects." I thought for a moment that he would tell us to get out. Instead, Dr. Welker let out a sigh. "The trouble with these bothersome people is that even after they're gone, they still cause trouble. The police interviewed me, but I didn't have anything useful to tell them. When I came out of the elevator that morning, Dr. Randall unlocked the door to her office and disappeared."

"You didn't see anyone else?" I asked.

"That strange woman that works for her arrived about the same time. I think Dorothy saw one of her patients, a middle-aged man, in the hall a few minutes later."

"We didn't see anyone except for Dr. Randall."

"There are always different people going into the other offices on our floor. It's rare that I recognize anyone." Dr. Welker frowned. "My practice hasn't been doing so well these last couple of years."

"Did you know Dr. Randall well?"

"We talked a few times. I admit I was jealous of her thriving practice. Though, the killer will no doubt be one of her patients." He tapped his pen on the desk. "Hypnosis can't solve everything."

Oh. Maybe I wasn't off the hook. I'd have to find a way to divert my desire to smoke if my hypnotic suggestion failed. Hypnosis had worked for her receptionist, at least for however long Jessica had worked for Dr. Randall.

"I wanted to stop smoking," El said, bringing me back from my thoughts.

"Yes, it's easy to see why you might think hypnosis would help." His face brightened. "Sometimes, it does seem better to manage the symptoms instead of dragging up all sorts of ideas that might make you feel worse."

I blew my nose.

The doctor looked at me and laughed. "You can't lie very well, either one of you."

"I hope that the police think the same," I said. "Who else has offices on this floor?"

"There's a marketing company down at the end of the hall. I've seen people coming out of their offices with signs and such, but I'm not sure exactly what they do." Dr. Welker opened up a drawer and brought out a small stack of papers. He handed it to El. "This is a directory of all the people with offices in the building. I never use it."

"Thanks so much."

"I don't know what good it will do you. The police questioned me, probably because they thought Dr. Randall and I competed for patients. But my patients are referred by their primary physicians. If the patients happened to all go to the same physicians that have agreements with me, she might have ended up taking some of my patients." The doctor suddenly frowned. "I wish everyone would stop wasting my time," he said and abruptly stood up.

His sudden change in attitude scared me. I realized that he might have been lying to us, a good strategy if he'd decided to take over Dr. Randall's blackmailing scheme.

He continued, "What a pain she was with her ads and that ridiculous suite she put in for her hypnosis treatments. Our local chapter of the APA talked about what a charlatan she was. She gets herself murdered, yet everyone still talks about her like she'd discovered a magic fix."

"I'm so sorry," I said and stood too. "We'll be going now. Thank you for your time."

El clutched the directory to her chest, perhaps afraid he might change his mind.

"That woman with her pink this and pink that. Get out. Get out before I call the police." The doctor's face turned bright red. A clump of his hair fell awkwardly to the side. He looked like he was going to have a heart attack.

Dorothy reappeared in the hall. "More reporters?"

"No, we aren't reporters." El edged her way around the doctor in the narrow hallway.

"Get out," Dr. Welker yelled again.

Dorothy herded us into the waiting room. "You best go."

"I don't know why he's so angry," El said. "He was friendly enough at first."

"It's been a long week," Dorothy replied as we exited the outer door.

I heard her twist the lock. When I tried the door again, it didn't budge.

We must add both of them to the list of suspects, Sherlock whispered.

Chapter 16

"That was strange," El said as we left the elevator.

I kept looking behind me. Part of me feared that Dr. Welker might follow us to the lobby. With all the unbelievable events that had occurred over the last couple of days, to *not* be afraid would have been stupid. I waited for the doctor to emerge from the stairway on our right.

His nurse would not allow him to leave his office, Sherlock whispered.

El walked carefully across the marble floor in her four-inch heels. "Does he have Alzheimer's or something?"

"Why do you wear those?" I'd never questioned her about her choice of shoes even though I wanted to many times. "Marble floors, cracks in sidewalks, there's an endless list of hazards. I can't see why looking like you do would be worth a broken ankle."

"I suppose you're right. But they are hard to give up." She pushed against the glass revolving door. El loved her shoes. Her closet full of expensive shoes must be worth a fortune.

"You know more about Alzheimer's than I do," El said taking my arm at the curb as we waited for a couple of cars to pass.

"So now I have Alzheimer's?" I snorted. El shrugged as if she didn't get what I meant, which of course she didn't because she didn't know about Sherlock. As far as memory served, multiple personalities had never been part of early Alzheimer's. Everything around me seemed threatening.

I knew a little about Alzheimer's. My research at the agency sometimes involved the disease. Obviously, not enough to diagnose anyone. But I was sure that Sherlock wasn't the result of an early case. I remembered everything from the last several days—except for the end of my session with Dr. Randall.

"I meant that Dr. Welker might have Alzheimer's not you," she said and pulled me out into the street. She looked closely at my face before she resumed her scan of the pavement for possible hazards.

"Probably not. Parkinson's?" I replied to her question.

"Would that make him dangerous?"

El seemed intrigued by the murder and investigation. Hanging around as my companion while I sorted out my life couldn't have been very stimulating. She probably missed those times when the regulatory timetables drove us, and the necessary spinning of the correct info in a positive way for the political appointees (as long as we were telling the truth) became a true art. All the people from the different agencies and firms we met while we analyzed their proposals had made life interesting.

The last couple of days had decidedly not been fun, especially learning about El's reason for talking me into going to the hypnotist.

"If someone planned Dr. Randall's death, Dr. Welker probably isn't our murderer. I mean, he might lose his temper, but I can't see him planning to kill anyone. Besides, Dorothy wouldn't let him keep a gun in the office," I stated. As surprising as the good doctor's actions had been, he didn't have a strong motive—unless he'd been blackmailed too.

"His nurse might not have known that he owned a gun. He could have slipped out of his office and knocked on Dr. Randall's private door." El looked back at the corner building. "We should talk to the other people on her floor sometime."

I suppose Dr. Welker wouldn't need a motive if his mood flipped like it did today.

An older woman was walking a cute, white poodle with a blue collar studded with shiny stones. The lady examined us and looked away. Across the street, a man in a shiny, three-piece brown or very dark olive-colored suit and an unbuttoned khaki overcoat flapping behind him walked briskly down the sidewalk. He appeared to take no interest in us at all. I was on edge, fearing any potential criminals pointing a gun at us in broad daylight.

Sherlock wasn't shy about speaking his mind. *I believe they would have to be fairly close to be accurate with a small firearm.*

If they owned a handgun, they could also have a rifle. In the movies, the marksman would cut a circle out of the glass to shoot their prey. Our killer probably wasn't that sophisticated—at least none of the suspects that I'd met or heard about would know how to do that. I looked up at the surrounding buildings.

The sun emerged from the clouds and felt warm on my face in the brisk autumn air. The weather could improve my mood even with a killer on the loose. A few red and yellow leaves tumbled across the sidewalk. Not far away, elegant houses marched down the block in a myriad of styles. Maple trees with their bright red leaves stood out among yellowing giants.

"Let's go back," she said. "Dorothy's probably given him a sedative or something. You are looking pale." El put a hand on my forehead. After a moment, she jumped back. "What was that?"

The twitch above my right eye was back. I'd had the same problem when I studied for midterms and finals in college as I spent the last week before my Thursday and Friday tests reading instead of sleeping. Curious that my reaction to my new non-smoking existence provoked the same reaction as sleep deprivation.

"You mean my twitch?" I snorted. "This not smoking thing seems to be playing havoc with my nervous system." Either that or worrying about El getting shot. Of course, I had other stuff going on too.

I really needed to tell her about Sherlock.

Perhaps another time, he said.

El cocked an eyebrow. "You didn't say anything about a twitch."

"Don't worry about it, I'm sure it will go away. After all, I've only been in the After Smoking Zone for a few days." Humor was a good way to deflect her interest. When I looked up, a man in a black hoodie was walking toward us.

"Very funny." She glanced back at the building across the street. "We can pump you full of caffeine at lunch."

As I watched the man in the hoodie, Mr. Randall appeared and walked to a blue sedan parked down the block. "Shh. Open the door."

I slid into my seat, closely mirrored by El. When Mr. Randall glanced back, I looked away and held my hand to my forehead as if I was shielding my eyes from the sun. He did a U-turn from his parking space and drove to the stop sign behind us. Following someone who might have killed his wife sounded exciting in a TV show. In real life, not so much. For the thousandth time in the last few days, I wondered what had possessed my friend.

The guy in the hoodie tore my attention away. We were sitting ducks if the new arrival was the killer. He walked past us without a glance. Why did so many people wear hoodies?

"Will he recognize you?" El asked as I tried to keep my face buried in a map from the glove compartment.

"I imagine so."

"It won't hurt to see where he's going as long as we're not too obvious."

"What if he killed Dr. Randall?" El's Mini might be too obvious. I would notice a black-bodied, white-topped Mini following me.

Ahead of us, Mr. Randall made his way to a Chinese restaurant on Wisconsin Avenue only about five blocks from his wife's office. He slid his rather old Audi into a convenient parking place. He jumped out with a brown briefcase and met an older Chinese gentleman who greeted him at the door.

"He's probably having lunch," I mused. My own stomach growled. I'd been nibbling more since I'd quit smoking and needed a food fix.

Mr. Randall was out of the restaurant in quick order and walked back the way we'd come to a *Copy Shop* on the opposite side of the street. There wasn't any need for us to follow him. He talked with the man at the counter before an older man—maybe the proprietor of the shop—appeared and handed Mr. Randall a small object that looked like a thumb drive.

"What do you want to bet those are his clients?"

A trim blond twenty or so years younger than Mr. Randall walked down the block. She stopped outside the *Copy Shop* and peered through the window. Our suspect seemed to sense her presence and gave her a wave. Outside, the young woman gave him a hug that lasted too long.

"Who is that woman?" I asked.

El made a face. "Are they going to make out in the middle of the street?"

Almost on cue, he leaned over and gave her a sloppy kiss on the cheek. The young woman hugged him again and took his arm. They took off in his dusty sedan together.

"Well, what do you think of that?" El unsnapped her seatbelt.

"Let's talk about it inside the restaurant." My stomach growled again. I shouldn't have been that hungry. A glance at my watch proved me wrong. It was already past twelve.

The steamed dumplings tasted great, and my twitching did subside after a couple of cups of dark tea. When I paused to look at our surroundings, I was surprised by the expensive decorations. They appeared to be the real thing, not knock-offs. In the full dining room, the waiters darted around between the tables in their white shirts and black pants, white aprons tied around their waists. No one seemed to be taking a particular interest in us. If I was waiting for an opportunity to kill someone, it wouldn't be in a Chinese restaurant like in some spy movie. I would wait in an alley along the route to our car. The killer would have at least a fifty-fifty chance to get away without anyone getting a good look at his face.

When the elderly gentleman who had talked to Mr. Randall approached our table, I did my best to hold his attention for more than the mandatory pleasantries. "I believe I saw a friend of mine stop to talk to you right before we came into your restaurant."

He bowed his head as if that was enough of an acknowledgment of my comment.

"Are you friends with Mr. Randall?"

"Oh yes, Mr. Randall. He is my accountant." The older man was clearly distressed. "He lost his wife recently." The plain statement said so much more than any drawn-out explanation.

El spoke, "Yes, we were acquainted with her too. It's very shocking."

"I would have liked to offer my condolences. He moved on so quickly I didn't get a chance, and he seemed to run into an acquaintance of his on the street," I added.

The man nodded his head and put up a hand with several fingers raised as he moved away from our table.

"What do you suppose that meant?" I asked while I poured myself another cup of tea.

"Either it was none of our business, or he was anxious to talk to the next table." El cocked her head to the side.

From the look on his face, our Chinese friend had decided not to tell us something.

Chapter 17

I wanted more caffeine, but El wanted to go back to Mr. Randall's office after we'd finished our food. She walked around the cracks in the street as if playing a childish game and ignored my protests. Inside, we didn't see any sign of Dr. Welker or Dorothy—or Mr. Randall for that matter. A small blessing since I wanted to take in our surroundings again in peace. And we were probably safe for now. If anyone wanted to shoot us, they'd had plenty of opportunities.

The Directory near the Wisconsin door of Dr. Randall's office building showed the same five entries we'd found on Dr. Welker's list. Take away Dr. Randall and Dr. Welker, two other companies (ACR Industries and FLM) occupied the same floor. There was also a firm called Precision Accounting.

El looked up. "Do you suppose that's Mr. Randall's firm?"

"There's an easy way to find out." My forehead twitched again. Muscles above my eye were twitching as well, which was freaky. I moved my eyebrows up and down a couple of times trying to make the twitch stop as we boarded the elevator.

"Fourth floor coming up," El said and pushed the button.

My forehead muscle, whatever it might be technically called (perhaps the Corrugator Supercilii) throbbed again. I tried raising one eyebrow, then both. I think my ears were moving too.

El laughed. "Are you going to wiggle your ears the whole time we're in there?"

We walked past 401 which was Dr. Randall's office. Yellow police tape crisscrossed both the door to the waiting room and the second private door. I guessed they were making sure that nobody else ducked into the office under the tape like I had.

El stood only a few feet away from the office across the hall. A small sign hanging perpendicular to the door said FLM. I wondered if Mr. Randall worked with the marketing firm.

"We can check it out it after the accounting firm."

"Did your forehead stop twitching?" She put her hand to my head like an old-fashioned damsel in distress.

My forehead resumed its normal repose. "I guess all those contortions do work."

Up ahead, the fluorescent lights under a white square panel flickered and went out.

"I don't like this," El said and stopped dead in her tracks.

The way in front of us was dark except for a slice of light coming from one narrow window across from the doors. Behind us, the panels that lit the hall were working just fine. The dark corridor didn't bother me. I strode past El and knocked on the door of Precision Accounting before I twisted the knob.

But I was glad that the waiting room was brilliantly lit. The room, much smaller than Dr. Randall's waiting room, measured only about eight by ten feet. A few beige chairs lined the walls, interrupted by a small glass window which a lady promptly slid to the side. Everyone else on this floor had a receptionist that talked to people in the waiting room.

"May I help you?" she asked.

I looked back at El. "Is this Mr. Randall's office?"

The receptionist pursed her lips. Her short, blond hair bounced when she shook her head from side-to-side. "You can't see him. He's not here."

"We're not reporters." El pushed me to the side. "My friend here knows him."

"Really?" She shook her head again. "Do you expect me to believe you?"

I suppose a reporter would say something like that. I put my shoulder to El's. "We were there when Dr. Randall was murdered."

"Wow, that must have been terrible," she leaned forward and lowered the volume of her voice, "What happened?"

"Dr. Randall hypnotized my friend," El said, "And for some reason, I fell asleep too."

"You're investigating the murder?" The receptionist stood up and held a finger up to her lips. She appeared at the door and walked out of the small office, closing the door behind her. "I came into the office that day too. Did the police question you?" She walked across the small reception area over the roughly woven carpet. His accounting firm had prospered if the carpet and furniture were any indication.

"Terrible," El said. "We weren't even awake, at least not for very long."

"I'm so sorry you had to go through that!" She looked sympathetic enough. Then, she held out her hand. "I'm Lucy, by the way. It's such a relief to talk to someone about the murder. We all have questions, but Mr. Randall told us he would appreciate us not talking to each other or the press about the murder."

"I'm Sissy and this is El," I answered as my friend shook her hand. "Why do you suppose he didn't want you to talk about her murder?

You should pay attention, Sherlock reminded me.

"I think he's afraid that more stories will get in the press I suppose. Mr. Randall wasn't even in the office that day." Lucy said as she sat down on a beige chair, identical to the ones in Dr. Randall's waiting room.

"I didn't see him either," I said. El looked at me as if I'd said something wrong.

We might have seen him if he was the other person in Dr. Randall's office, Sherlock whispered.

"Who did you see?" El asked, the proverbial dog on the scent.

I didn't have much hope that we would be able to obtain enough information from Lucy to make any difference, but she seemed anxious to gossip about the murder

"I wish I saw someone other than you go into Dr. Randall's office." Lucy leaned closer. "I saw you two arrive because I'd gone out to pick up coffee for me and Alice, Mr. Randall's accounting assistant."

"That's actually very helpful for us to put together a timeline. We exited the elevator very close to ten. I do remember you now."

"When did Dr. Randall arrive?" Lucy asked, obviously enjoying the conversation.

"Nine o'clock. It's safe to say that's the same time that her receptionist, Dr. Welker, and Dorothy arrived. Somewhere, between nine and ten, Dorothy saw a patient arrive, and that fits with what Jessica said."

I liked this girl. I also liked the idea of figuring out the sequence of events. Sherlock had said something about figuring out the order of what happened that day.

Lucy put a white hand over mine. "Is Jessica, okay?"

"She seemed fine when we took her out to lunch." I felt a little guilty. We only had worried about ourselves. Mr. Randall lost his wife. Jessica lost her employer and friend.

"At ten, we arrived, and you left for coffee," El said taking notes again. "When did you get back?"

"I'm pretty careful to take only fifteen minutes for each break even though I can take more. Mr. Randall doesn't watch us the same way Dr. Randall watched Jessica." Lucy's eyes widened. "I didn't mean anything."

"Jessica complained?" I asked.

"I didn't mean that Jessica didn't like her. She always talked about how Dr. Randall helped her lose weight."

She might have resented the doctor's control over her.

I had hoped Sherlock might stay silent during the rest of the conversation. It was hard enough focusing on the interview with Lucy when I didn't feel well.

You and El have done a bang-up job. I commend your efforts.

Sherlock had some nerve sitting back there evaluating every word I said. My forehead began to twitch again.

Lucy looked at her watch which I took as a signal that we should leave.

El handed Lucy one of her cards. "Do call if you remember anything that might help us."

We left the office not much better off than before. A timeline would be helpful, but right now, Mr. Randall seemed to have a strong motive—if he did have a mistress. Once our police detective took a look at Dr. Randall's expenses, there might be irregularities.

No one was in the marketing office across the hall. Lucy had told us that they only used the space when they had banners or signs to make. The firm's main location was down the block. The only other office was a legitimate massage therapist. According to Lucy, she hadn't been in the day of the murder.

"You see, I had this cold," the massage therapist told us, brushing back some stray blond hairs. I wanted to ask her where she was from but that didn't seem appropriate. She might not want people to know for some reason like immigration or stereotypes.

I do not understand why you worry about the privacy of people who might have murdered Dr. Randall and El's friend.

Not everyone we interview is the killer. Just because we're investigating a murder doesn't mean we should be rude. If El had heard me, she'd thought I'd gone insane. She seemed to think I was rude most of the time, at least that's what it had sounded like when she talked to the EMT.

Whoever killed Dr. Randall and probably Marcus too, is far beyond caring about manners.

Marcus would agree with Sherlock, especially since he probably couldn't afford to pay his blackmailer. I could only imagine one reason he'd become a target, the killer had contacted him, asking for more money. Detective Kirkland's suspicions had probably been right about someone wanting to take over Dr. Randall's blackmailing scheme.

My forehead throbbed making me forget about the interview at hand.

"I give you a massage?" she asked. "Your face does not obey you."

El laughed.

Ingrid's face reddened. "I'm sorry. My English is not good."

"Ingrid, I didn't laugh at you. I'm sorry! Sissy quit smoking, and she's having a few side effects."

This time the massage therapist laughed too. "Yes, the body does not like change. You will like this not smoking. Costs too much, and the smell," she pinched her nose.

I snorted. "You're right. Will a massage get rid of my twitch?"

"Let us try. My appointment for this hour cancelled out at the last minute. Murder is not good for business. I think he didn't want to come to a building where a murder has happened." She picked up a couple of pure white towels from a table in her office. "You want massage too?" she asked El.

"Next time," El said.

I'd never had a massage before. Ingrid found knots that had formed in the muscles of my shoulders and neck. The ones in my shoulders were difficult for her to smooth out.

"Did Dr. Randall ever get a massage?" I asked. Ingrid pushed down on a muscle in my back that should have hurt since she attacked it with such vigor, but didn't. I felt a twinge just above the shoulder blade before the muscle relaxed. She switched to my left side. Farther down, other muscles needed her attention.

"Oh yes, she came to me every week."

Perhaps she told Ingrid something important, Sherlock whispered.

I doubted that Dr. Randall had gone on and on about her blackmailing scheme to an office neighbor, but it was worth a shot to investigate.

"What did she like to talk about?" I asked, trying to sound casual.

"The police, they want to know such things. Did she talk about her husband? Any of her patients? I told them no." Ingrid slapped my right shoulder. That smarted.

"I didn't think she would."

"Her husband comes to me sometimes when he's sore from playing handball."

Indeed, what is this handball?

I ignored Sherlock's remark. Mr. Randall kept cropping up all over the place.

"I don't suppose he said anything to you?"

"He is a quiet man. Falls asleep while he gets his massage. I think he cares about his wife." She moved up to my neck. "He asked me what he should get his wife for her birthday."

I jerked awake. The rhythm of her hands had made me sleepy.

"See, easy to fall asleep when you get a massage." Ingrid rubbed more oil onto her hands.

"What is that smell?" I mumbled. The cushion around the hole provided for my face had been covered by a towel-like cloth that partially covered my mouth.

"Rosemary. You like this scent? This is the same oil that Dr. Randall liked. I will miss her," she said before she started smoothing my muscles again, this time working in longer strokes.

I recognized the scent. But I'd met Dr. Randall for the first time on the day she was murdered, and Ingrid said the doctor hadn't been in that day.

If she had been in that day, your detective would have unearthed the fact by now.

Dr. Randall entered the building at nine. It seemed unlikely she had a massage before we arrived at ten.

Oil residue may still be present on her clothing or furniture. Do you remember smelling the scent in her office?

The well-ordered pink office, sunlight streaming into the room, the terrible figure outlined in yellow on the floor, and yes, by her desk I'd smelled that same scent.

Ingrid finished by rubbing my head, starting at my temples and ending on my shoulders. The tension in my shoulders disappeared.

Most of the people we'd talked to had strong opinions about Dr. Randall, but Ingrid had liked her. I imagined that blackmailing could change a person's opinion.

"What did you tell him to buy for her?" With all that extra money rolling in, she must have had everything.

"Something pink," she said smiling.

When I tried to pay Ingrid for the massage, she waved me away.

"First time is free. You come back when you get that twitch again," she said and handed me her card.

I had no idea when my twitch stopped. First, it was getting stronger and faster by the minute and then poof, it was gone. The massage was the best solution. I would want to come in for another massage if my twitch returned, maybe even if it didn't. My muscles had stored up all my nervous tension.

Our trip had not provided us with much information. We had no evidence to support our hypothesis that Dr. Welker or Dorothy—or anyone else for that matter—had decided to take over Dr. Randall's blackmail business. We still didn't know why Marcus had been killed.

Chapter 18

Even though Mr. Randall appeared to have a mistress, and even though I had questioned my ability to judge a person's character by looking at them, I had this nagging feeling that my first impression of Mr. Randall had been right. I still didn't believe he had murdered his wife even though I had no evidence to support my belief. Maybe I believed in his innocence because I believed he had loved his wife.

When I suggested to El that we visit Mr. Randall tomorrow, she whole-heartedly agreed. "I'm glad you're not freaking out about me being in danger."

If the killer was anxious to eliminate her, wouldn't they have tried by now?

The culprit may be exercising more patience than they have shown in the past.

"Why don't you stay at my place again?"

The traffic became much heavier, as it tended to do at odd times, bunching up on the Beltway as the cars caught up to the slower traffic ahead. A group of them arrived out of nowhere, crowding into our lane before the merge onto the Georgia Avenue ramp.

"Don't look so worried. Let's go to my place, and I can pick up a change of clothes."

"Hector and Achilles need attention too. It wouldn't hurt for us to stray from our normal routine. Let's go out to dinner in Bowie."

The fiery sun sunk towards the horizon. The tops of the cars in the parking lot of El's condo shone with an orange glow. Shadows stretched to the east from the buildings, providing a safe hiding place for a hooded figure. I looked and looked before I let El get out of the car. Finally, I walked up to the front door of the building myself to see if anyone looked suspicious. When I saw it was clear, I went back to escort her inside.

"You would think you were an action movie hero the way you're checking out my building," El said with a nervous laugh. "C'mon."

Straight ahead an old lady held the elevator door for us. Before the doors of the elevator closed, an elderly gentleman in a long overcoat still touched by the sun's golden rays appeared walking across the beige marble floor. He looked harmless enough, but I let the elevator doors close.

You forget that if the killer is one of Dr. Randall's other patients, we might not recognize them.

A bodyguard's job was hard.

El quickly unlocked her door. No one ever seemed to be around in any of the hallways we'd been in lately—a good thing I suppose.

I wondered if we projected our fear. If I felt that from another person, I don't know how I would react. But it was better to have people around, wasn't it? The killer wouldn't want witnesses. Each time, they'd caught their victim alone.

They needed to be close enough to make sure they hit their mark.

Fear and anger, laughter, and joy. All human emotions are contagious. Watchfulness does not translate into fear. You, however, may be making others uncomfortable because of your scrutiny. I have experienced such a reaction myself. You are correct about the firearm too. The one who killed Dr. Randall and El's friend will not be shooting at her from a distance.

I wanted to laugh. Sherlock had the capacity to annoy a great many people by analyzing their every move and word, if they only knew he was there.

People do not like to be so well understood.

If we really did, we wouldn't keep so many secrets.

Ah, yes. Your privacy.

Our government protected our privacy and took it away at the same time. They wouldn't be able to protect us without information.

The British had the same kind of dilemma when I was alive.

They probably dealt with the same thing since they still had a royal family. We didn't have one in the States.

Yes, of course. Although I found their ways perplexing at times, I always accepted the upper class. Your lack of a monarchy is your loss. The English world would not be the same without a royal family.

The cats seemed anxious for attention when we got to Aunt Pet and Uncle Roger's house. They were very self-sufficient most of the time, but seemed to be missing their owners more. Hector must have been lounging on top of the bookcase when I unlocked the door, because he jumped into my arms.

El was impressed. "I've never seen a cat do that before. Those little dogs, the ones that yap a lot, probably jump into people's arms all the time."

"I suppose they're lonely after three weeks."

Hector purred so loudly it vibrated through his whole body. His pale blue eyes looked up from that chocolate-colored face of his.

"Why don't we get takeout? Pet and Roger won't care as long as we clean up." El still looked strained.

My stress quotient was about nil because of Ingrid's massage. The next time a part of me was stiff, I would definitely book an appointment.

"Let's stay here tonight." My aunt and uncle's house felt like a refuge from all the craziness that pursued us.

"Would they mind?" El asked.

"They know that I'm taking care of the cats this week. And they're always telling me I can stay over if I like since it's a long drive from Silver Spring."

A smile lit up El's face, something I hadn't seen often enough lately.

Naturally. You must never forget how human we all are. When a person is easily frightened, you must not disquiet them. When they are gullible, you will regret taking advantage of that trust. I learned some hard lessons during my lifetime.

I was about to ask him to tell me what happened when El spoke.

"What kind of food would you like?" She was going through a basket of menus she'd found on the counter. Aunt Pet kept them all together along with the coupons.

We finally settled on Chinese and HBO. Exhausted, I made the guest room up for El before dinner. Sleep evaded me after I snuggled into the fresh sheets in the single bed in Aunt Pet's sewing room. Random thoughts about guns and blackmail kept going through my head. Who owned a handgun? Only Rudy protested that he didn't have a gun. Dorothy wouldn't have let Dr. Welker keep a gun in his office. At least I didn't think she would since she'd been so protective of the aging doctor.

And the blackmail was a mystery too. Rudy had paid his latest installment the day of Dr. Randall's murder. Jessica said something about looking in Dr. Randall's inner office, the room where Dr. Randall had been killed, to see if he'd gone. She must have guessed he was there. Did they all deliver their money directly to Dr. Randall? Nobody would write a check, would they? Checks were so easily traced. I bet she preferred cash.

You, we, need our rest. If you start pacing about, you won't go to sleep for hours. That is my experience. My dependence on cocaine was not as habitual as Watson thought. I merely used it to relieve my sleepless nights.

Sherlock was right about the pacing. If he hadn't spoken, I would have gone downstairs to romp with the cats, acting like I was doing something instead of working off nervous energy.

Tomorrow you can ask these questions again. This acquaintance of Mr. Tessmeyer, the one who gave him the referral to Dr. Randall, we must interview him no matter how distasteful that might be.

We would be ready after a good night's sleep, if sleep would come. I hoped that the same wouldn't be true of the killer.

This person who so crudely settled their problem by shooting Dr. Randall will give themselves away, I assure you. They acted rashly when they attacked El's friend. Perhaps he tried to contact them directly. And they will act rashly again.

I wasn't so sure I agreed with him. Whoever killed Dr. Randall had a gun, and a can of spray paint to sabotage the security cameras. That sounded like a well-planned attack to me as if they'd watched a lot of mysteries on TV.

I do not understand how such a bulky device would work.

My eyelids were heavy. Tomorrow, I thought, I will remember what I've forgotten about the day of the murder.

When I pulled up the memory, the room still appeared to be draped in shadows even after Detective Kirkland demonstrated otherwise.

I let sleep take me.

Day 9
Chapter 19

El insisted that we visit Mr. Randall first. I didn't blame her for wanting to put off our interview with this Williamson character. I didn't want to visit him either.

Human nature makes us want to believe the most distasteful people are responsible for all the world's woes.

No matter what El thought of him, I didn't believe Mr. Randall was dangerous. He would be a better person to talk to first. I called him and made an appointment for after lunch. The man sounded normal enough on the phone; even seemed sorry about Marcus' death which surprised me.

The address wasn't hard to find. They lived in a beautiful old colonial with a broad, white portico not far from Rudy Tessmeyer's house. The yard was well kept, and the grass lush even though it was November. Someone had shaped the evergreens under the windows, so they appeared symmetrical, matching the long row of evergreens that marked the border of the front yard and the sidewalk. El and I walked down the winding brick path to the front door.

Harvey Randall opened the door before my hand could reach the bell. "Hello?" His voice sounded friendly enough, slightly lower in pitch

"Do you mind if we ask you some questions?" My own voice wasn't as steady as I would have liked.

The look on his face softened. "I forgot you were coming."

I was surprised when El stepped forward and put her hand on his arm. At first, I thought she was being kind. Then I realized she was trying to get him to move. After he stepped aside to let us in, El slipped through the door, and I passed within inches of Mr. Randall when I followed her. His red hair stuck out, and the buttons of his pressed white shirt weren't lined up with the buttonholes on the other side. The poor man hadn't even been able to dress properly.

Not every murderer is a slick mastermind or a ruffian, Sherlock reminded me.

Even if Mr. Randall had killed his wife, I wasn't sure that meant he would kill anyone else. Mr. Randall looked up to meet my gaze. He was only two feet away from me, if that. As I surveyed his face, I found he didn't look surprised. His eyes looked directly into mine, and his mouth sagged, accentuating his thin lips. He might be a sad man with the intelligence and curiosity to want to find out more about the murder of his wife.

You cannot tell such things from only looking at a man, Sherlock said. I ignored Sherlock's comments. Naturally, the entire living room was pink. Two couches formed a U-shape before the dark pink bricks of the fireplace. Artistic glassware stood in a tall, built-in cabinet to the right side. Even the silk flowers on the long dark wood table were pink. I snorted again forgetting about the seriousness of the situation. I should have acted with more decorum than usual.

He wiped tears from his face and smiled. "It is too much, but I've grown used to it."

El scowled at me.

We followed Mr. Randall into the kitchen, tiled in black and white tiles on the walls and floor. Even the cabinets were painted white with black trim.

"Do you like Columbian coffee?" Mr. Randall asked.

"Dark roast, if you have it." When it came to coffee, Sherlock voiced strong opinions.

"Good choice. I favor dark roast as well."

"Why didn't she make your kitchen pink?"

"This is one of my rooms," he said starting the coffee maker.

I tried to remember that we were here because he might have killed his wife.

Have you forgotten about the young blond woman we saw kissing him?

El hadn't been derailed from the purpose of our visit. "I understand that you weren't in the office the day your wife was shot."

He frowned. "Yes, that's what I told the police."

"Why?"

Mr. Randall seemed deep in thought. Maybe he'd been there and hadn't admitted it to the police. "If only I had been there, I might have been able to save her."

I wasn't prepared to see his grief. It didn't seem that long since I'd lost my Harry. "Detective Kirkland seems to be focusing on other aspects of the investigation."

"You mean the blackmailing," El shot back. She may have felt bad when she saw how upset he was, but her voice was the same one she had used on Mr. Tessmeyer the first time we met.

"I should have stopped all of that nonsense sooner. She promised me that she was going to stop. I was surprised when Detective Kirkland said that someone had paid her off that day."

"Rudy Tessmeyer did go into her office to pay her the day she was shot," El said ruthlessly.

I reminded myself that others had been hurt by Dr. Randall. We had no way to know if Mr. Randall had been involved in the blackmailing scheme.

"We moved here to escape one of her patients. But it's not so easy when a patient is so very dependent on their analyst."

Dr. Welker did say he thought the killer could be one of her patients.

All the people she blackmailed were patients so that doesn't narrow the field much. Even though Dr. Randall had been the victim, she'd also been the blackmailer.

He nodded. "I understand why you find it hard to believe that she was also victimized, but it happens all the time. Patients become dependent on their analysts, want more attention than they can receive in a one-hour appointment. Some of them rang our house, swearing and calling her the worst names. They would call for weeks before they would stop." He wiped his brow. "I know it doesn't excuse her own wrongdoing."

"I don't think anyone who was being blackmailed would have harassed your wife." El put her hands on her hips.

"You're right if you think like a well-balanced person, but it still happened. Psychiatrists often have that kind of problem. I answered the phone at all hours for years. The Sunday morning calls bothered me most. Even when we changed our number, moved to another suburb, they still found us. Nothing shocks me now. But I'm her husband. I should have protected her."

El was looking through the cabinets for coffee cups.

"The coffee cups are in the next cupboard to your left," a voice said from the doorway. It was same young woman we'd seen with Randall before.

"There you are," he said. A smile lit his face. "I thought you might be taking a nap."

"I couldn't sleep. Every time I close my eyes, I see Mom."

"Mom?" El said softly.

Indeed, was all Sherlock said.

We had expected the worst and gone too far this time.

I offered my hand to the young woman. "I'm Sissy and this is my friend El. We were at the office when your mother was…"

It was too late. Tears filled her eyes and started running down her fair cheeks.

"Oh, my dear Louise." Her father pulled her into an embrace. There was love here. Dr. Randall—Phillipa, I reminded myself—had been his wife and her mother.

"Would you mind coming back another time?" Mr. Randall said.

"I'm so sorry we've intruded." El hung her head.

"It's not your fault. Come by tomorrow if you can," Mr. Randall said, holding onto his daughter.

We nodded and left.

After we were back in the car, El said, "I can't believe we thought she was his mistress."

"Made perfect sense to me. We were looking for a motive to pin on him."

El deftly maneuvered our way around the one-way streets back to Wisconsin Avenue.

The traffic was getting heavy now that we were back on the Beltway. It would be a while before El would speak again. When she'd been negative at work, she had the excuse that she was doing her job. I hadn't seen her react so harshly since we retired. She had been so kind to me.

We need to talk to this Williamson now, Sherlock persisted.

The way Rudy talked about him, Williamson sounded wimpy and nasty. I wasn't sure if that made him dangerous or not. Maybe he could be if he were cornered.

"Does Williamson live in Gaithersburg?" El asked, as if reading my thoughts.

"Yes. If we go now, we'll be there early."

"Let's get it over with."

I nodded. Catching Williamson off-guard might give us an advantage.

"You want to take this exit and put the address in the GPS." The sign for Georgia Avenue was in view. I didn't know how to get to Williamson's house except he'd said it was out in a wooded area.

"I'm glad we're going together." El was still staring at the road ahead.

We'd spent a lot of time driving around this week. I wanted to ask her if she was okay, but thought better of it. Marcus might still be on her mind.

I still loved Harry, too. He was gone wherever patient, loving people went. I would take care of El the way she'd taken care of me when I'd lost him.

Empathy comes through in your thoughts, even sympathy, Sherlock said, *Although I like how you do not let your finer sensibilities interfere with your logic. Women of my day were not so.*

They probably didn't voice their minds. If they were chastised at every turn, it wouldn't be so hard to act demure, even brainless.

Do I detect some ill humor? You are not inferring that I was mistaken in my analysis. He stated the latter as if it was the truth. Sherlock could command all he liked and yes, sometimes take over my body without my consent, but he could not dictate my opinions. I pushed him as far back from my thoughts as I could until I couldn't feel his presence. My temper was heating up, and I wouldn't have been able to speak silently if he'd decided to duke it out with me.

Williamson's house was, indeed, out in a heavily wooded area on a large lot that stretched down into a ravine. A tiny stream appeared to run under the wooden fence to our left all the way to the stockade-like fence on the right. Beyond the trees stretched to the crest of a large hill. A mixture of oak and birch, sprinkled with dark green pine trees and a few maples still partially covered by red and yellow leaves.

The leaves on the ground were layered like the pages of a book, flat and almost symmetrical. Some of them played in the wind, getting caught in the sudden gusts that had started once we were out on the country road. The day was so fresh, the sun shining brightly, it was a shame to go inside.

El pulled on my elbow. She smiled even as if she believed that interviewing this guy wouldn't be as bad as we expected.

If I'd wanted a cigarette, I would have had an excuse to linger in the driveway. Now, the smoke would be noxious. When I'd met with our detective, the smoke from his cigarette had smelled dirty. I am in control, I said like a mantra. And strangely enough, I was.

"Are you coming?" El looked very tired in the bright sunshine. The little lines around her eyes she so carefully dabbed with her special cream looked very deep, as if the skin underneath had cracked.

Only one car, a black Explorer, was parked in the driveway. El had parked her black and white Mini behind it, blocking the only exit. I wasn't worried that Williamson would want to jump into his car and drive away. We were the ones that might need a quick exit strategy.

I stopped in my tracks.

"What?" She wrinkled up her face.

"We may not be safe in there. Look out back. He must have acres of land. And the neighbors aren't home." The houses on either side of his were dark; and no cars were in their driveways.

"They're probably at work," she said, nodding at the house to our left. "Why did he say he would be home? I thought we were going to meet him in a public place?"

"I don't remember." Agreeing to come here was another one of my random acts, in a long line of random acts which hadn't gotten me killed, yet.

"You probably said yes, just to get the phone call over with as soon as possible." El's brow wrinkled. She knew me too well.

Phone conversations were pretty close to the top of my list of things that I didn't like to do, with the exception of my overseas chats with Aunt Pet.

"Let's do this," she said from the porch and knocked on the heavy oak door.

There was a small rectangular window at eye level. Inside I could see a grand piano halfway across the expanse of the open floor plan. Beyond the piano, the wooden floor stretched to a room with a view of the trees in the back of the property.

"Guess he decided he didn't want to talk to us." I started to leave the narrow porch when I heard the door creak open.

El had tried the knob.

"I don't think that means you should walk right into his house." My imagination took off. He could kill an intruder in his home and call it self-defense.

"He's probably downstairs or in the bathroom."

"Let's leave." I had a bad feeling about this. Any excuse would do. I certainly wouldn't want strangers wandering around my house when I was in the bathroom.

"Mr. Williamson?" she yelled through the door. She sounded like a nice neighbor who was announcing her presence.

The house was too quiet.

"Does he have another car?" That would explain why he wasn't answering the door, but not why it was left unlocked.

El stepped onto the light-colored stone floor. The irregularly shaped stones were laid out almost touching each other. It must have taken the installer forever to figure out the right arrangement for the stones. A pegged rack was on the wall next to the door.

"Mr. Williamson?"

The entry way was maybe ten by twelve feet, decorated with large plants in the far corners—banana, by the look of them, with long floppy leaves and thick stems. A long table with a distinctive grain and a slightly irregular shape was visible through another doorway, and I could see wall ovens through another archway to our left.

El was already in the room directly across from the door, walking across the dark oak floor. The shiny black grand piano was now to her left. "Let's look around."

"You must be nuts. Come back here." The words were barely out of my mouth before I heard another voice.

"Should I call the police?" A thin, mousey-looking man was standing in a hallway to my right.

"I called you." The words tumbled out of my mouth.

"Yes," was the only response.

"We have an appointment."

"You do have an appointment with me. Which does not give you carte blanche to take a look around as your friend had the gall to put it." He sneezed into a handkerchief. "I would call it breaking and entering."

"There was entering, but no breaking," El said. She was usually the facilitator, smoothing out the rough spots. But she'd had a rough time of it, so I wasn't going to push her.

"I do apologize," I said.

He focused his attention on me. "I've been a little off lately. All those grasses my neighbors like to plant don't agree with me—allergies, you see. But what can you do with no homeowner's association to complain too? Anyway. You mentioned Rudy." He blew his nose and led us into a seating arrangement to our right that had a huge gray modular sofa with black and gray striped chairs and pillows that matched on the sofa.

Both El and I chose the black, square-shaped chairs while Williamson sprawled on the couch and crossed his long thin legs.

"Mr. Tessmeyer said that you recommended Dr. Randall."

"I am so sorry about what happened to her. She seemed like a perfectly wonderful woman even though she always dressed in pink."

El was not to be denied. Sure, we'd been wrong about Mr. Randall's daughter. That didn't mean Rudy was wrong about Williamson. "A nice woman who liked to blackmail her patients. What went wrong, did you have to fork over one of your buddies because you needed the fifty grand for a piano?"

Williamson jumped up and threw the blue fake-fur pillow he'd cradled under his arm across the room.

"Setting another person up for blackmail must be against the law," I added before I realized I was on my feet too. "You're an accomplice."

'You didn't tell us she blackmailed you." An icy calm had settled over El. He wouldn't find any mercy in her. Her previous mistake had not diluted her anger.

"She tried." He sat down and stared at the glass table in front of him. The natural wood boughs that were crisscrossed to form legs for the table formed a frame around his knobby knees.

"And you didn't have the money, so you killed her," I said.

He glared at me. "How come you know so much? The cops were already here. They asked the same thing, only you aren't asking, are you? You're the old biddies who were in the office when she was killed? I've got an alibi. Lots better than yours, I bet."

We were, but if we acknowledged that we didn't have an alibi, he would be interrogating us, not the other way around. The only sound was the wind pushing the leaves through the trees outside. Finally, he looked away.

"I was at my sister's if you must know. Not a hard story to check out since her cleaning lady—the one who hates me—was there that day. Beatrice, she doesn't like my jokes."

Nobody would like this guy's jokes.

"That doesn't mean you couldn't hire someone to do it." El had sat down on the edge of the sofa as if she was ready to spring off her seat again.

"With what? I'm not exactly flush. That's why I had to give her Rudy. He could afford to pay," Williamson sneered. "All those little rich kids at school. They never had to earn a cent. And when they did, somebody was always setting them up with a cushy job."

Imagining the poor kid, probably on a scholarship, surrounded by privileged kids wasn't so hard for me. I had money from my parents in a trust they'd set-up, but I didn't get it until after I was out of college.

"How did you end up going to Dr. Randall? Did someone refer you?" I asked.

That is an excellent question. The blackmail trail may be the key to solving the murder.

"My problem wasn't as serious as Marcus' addiction." Williamson glanced nervously outside before he slumped on the couch.

"You didn't tell us you knew Marcus," El said.

He doesn't want to tell us how he found out about your hypnotist.

179

He considered her for a moment. "You must have been his girlfriend," he said

"I was his *friend*."

"Leave it to Marcus to get the pretty girl. Did you know that he'd run through most of his parent's money? I'm sure he didn't tell you that he was almost broke."

"I don't value a person that way."

"Sure, you don't."

"Who set you up?" I asked loudly. That startled him.

"That would be yet another school buddy."

"Tell us who," I persisted.

"I can't do that." He frowned.

"Do you think he killed Marcus?" The man openly stared at me. "I'm not the detective."

Outside, the wind picked up leaves off a path turning them into a miniature cyclone. Clouds had blown in while we were inside, replacing the welcome sunshine.

Tears filled El's eyes. She was done.

However, I wasn't. "Did you tell the police who recommended Dr. Randall to you?"

Williamson shook his head. "I'm glad that I can work at home. I'm safe here if I don't stand in front of the windows."

Both Dr. Randall and Marcus, I reminded myself, had been shot with a handgun at close range.

He doesn't know, Sherlock said. *He doesn't know what kind of gun was used.*

He wasn't the killer.

"Who set you up?" I demanded.

All the spite in Williamson seemed to drain away. "Jim Parker, he works at a bank in Bethesda. I was looking for a sympathetic soul who could help me get a loan for my business. After I took a smoking break during our discussion, he recommended Dr. Randall."

"Do you have any idea how many other people she blackmailed?"

Williamson screwed up his face again. "Get the hell out of my house and don't come back."

Pushing him more hadn't been a good strategy. We both made a quick exit this time, leaving him to cower in his house.

Outside, the first drops of rain hit us like pellets as we rushed to the car. The wind rocked El's Mini from side to side as if it wanted to fling us over the house into the woods. Brown oak leaves caught in the blast plastered the driver's side windows of the car.

I should have been happy that it wasn't cold enough to snow. If the temperature had already dropped, we might have had a hard time driving back to Silver Spring. As it was, El didn't want to drive because of the wind. I slid into the driver's seat.

As I drove away, I wondered what we should do next.

Williamson gave us the name of who told him about Dr. Randall. He didn't tell us if this Parker had also been blackmailed.

Detective Kirkland must have found out about Williamson's link to Rudy and Marcus. He might even know if Williamson had given other referrals to Dr. Randall.

We decided not to tell your detective that we knew about the blackmail.

I could change my mind, couldn't I?

And your constable can decide that we're dealing with two different killers.

Marcus had known drug dealers. From what El had mentioned earlier, he'd visited Dr. Randall last spring. If her treatment had worked as well for him as it had for me, his problem would have been resolved, unless the people he'd known from that less-reputable life hadn't been anxious for him to escape their grip.

These drugs were easy enough to procure in London.

They are illegal here. I let Sherlock digest that information.

The storm seemed to be almost over, although large drops still struck the car. The surrounding buildings on Georgia Avenue were blocking the worst of the wind. To our left, there was a thick stand of trees stretching across the hills. Then to our right, the wind came unobstructed across the flat fields and slammed against the car making me grip the steering wheel more tightly.

I had no doubt that, if Sherlock really had been using drugs in the late nineteenth century in London, he knew they did not bring out the best in people. The people Marcus had known and abandoned might have feared that he would give them away. Marcus seemed to have gone to great lengths to make sure that others didn't find out about his addiction.

Indeed. These other associates might well be responsible for both Dr. Randall's and Marcus' deaths.

If that was true, El could still be in danger.

Day 10
Chapter 20

Saturday didn't seem like a good day to visit a bank. I said as much while I made toast for El. The lobby would be filled with working folks who needed help with loans or new accounts.

A nice day at home or Aunt Pet's house sounded better. Hector and Achilles wouldn't mind the company. I wanted to burrow in for the rest of the weekend since the weatherman had predicted snow early Sunday morning. In our part of the country, we would probably lose our mobility for at least a day even though the snowfall usually started to melt the day after it fell, sometimes even on the same day. It would be easier to visit on Monday.

"He's in the office," El said after she finished her call. She looked professional with her neatly-styled wing of hair flying off the left side of her head and her casual black outfit. Leave it to her to fill every spare minute of the day. She was too energetic, even for her.

"You want to take it easy today?" I asked.

She might get in trouble if I let her go by herself. Marcus' death had shaken her and, in a knee-jerk reaction, her obsession to find Marcus' killer was consuming her. Her single-mindedness, once so valuable at work, wasn't an asset now. Dr. Randall's fate could end up being her own, but it didn't seem to matter to her.

Dr. Randall's murder is where it all started.

How can we be so sure? Kirkland told us he hadn't received the ballistics report for Marcus' murder.

Everything revolves around her. Sherlock said it in such a way that I imagined him shrugging his skinny shoulders. *What is this ballistics?*

I pulled up my own personal definition.

Ahh. Very interesting, indeed. If the bullets match, the murders are related, according to Detective Kirkland. I trust his judgement.

Ironic, considering he had once told me he mistrusted policemen.

Your memory serves you well. He appears to be quite perceptive, unlike the constabulary of my time. Did you never read the tales of my exploits recorded by Dr. Watson? However, without the proper laboratory equipment, we could not achieve the same results as Detective Kirkland. And I do not imagine that he would let us see any casings found at the scene.

I was glad that Sherlock wouldn't be conducting tests in my condo.

When I looked up, El had eaten her toast during my conversation with Sherlock. She was still watching me.

"You've been acting funny ever since Dr. Randall hypnotized you," she said in a manner-of-fact kind of way.

Perhaps this is the time to tell your friend about me.

El seemed relaxed. If I told her about Sherlock, she might freak out.

"What's going on?" she asked.

I didn't want to lie to her. She'd told me her secret, after all. Time for me to tell her mine.

"Do you believe in reincarnation?" I asked.

Her eyes widened. "I remember you telling me reincarnation was a bunch of baloney."

"Once I tell you what happened, you might think differently." I looked down at my plate, waiting for some help from Sherlock. He chose this moment to keep his peace, leaving me to fend for myself.

"Okay, this should be good." El brushed a crumb from her sweater and crossed her arms.

I did start at the beginning. I told her how Sherlock had surfaced during the hypnosis.

"How do you know the voice is Sherlock Holmes? I mean, why is everybody a famous person in their previous life? I suppose it's a good sign he's not Cleopatra." El laughed.

I could tell she didn't believe a word I said. She watched my reaction and frowned as if I'd made fun of her.

Let me talk to her.

He'd never asked my permission before. Impressed, I gave my consent. That subtle shift in the way I perceived myself meant he'd taken over in a much politer way.

"I am Sherlock Holmes," we said.

El stared blankly.

"Believe me. This fine lady and I are connected in some way. We are unsure how our current condition occurred. According to the information that Sissy looked up on her mechanical device she calls a laptop, there are no recorded experiences of one life talking to another. It is possible it occurred because Dr. Randall asked to speak to Sissy's inner self." His assumption surprised me even though I thought that myself.

"Sissy, can I talk to you?" El asked.

Sherlock gave a mental nod, and I took over.

"I'm here."

"Are you serious?" She clearly thought the whole thing was a joke.

"I would have told you sooner, but I expected him to go away."

El shook her head and laughed. After all she'd been through, she didn't want to accept this. She'd be more likely to believe I had two heads. Expletive-deletive.

"How can I prove that I'm serious?"

"You *are* serious?"

"More than you could ever imagine."

I thought she would be more understanding.

It seemed easier for El to watch some strange lady on a talk show have a psychic experience than see me haunted by Sherlock Holmes. There had to be a way to convince her.

"Is it so hard to believe that we live different lives?"

"There are an infinite number of things that can happen in the universe." She put her hands on her hips. "Is this payback?"

Our conversation was not going well.

I will try to make her understand.

No, I should do this. I know her best.

"I know it sounds like a bad joke," I said. "The day after Dr. Randall's murder, I didn't remember everything. Sherlock started talking, and I thought someone was playing a joke on me. I had this hysterical moment before I looked behind the couch and everywhere you might be hiding."

"Me? Why did it have to be me?" She looked hurt but waited for my response.

"You're the only one besides Aunt Pet who has a key to my condo. You're the one who talks about all these impossible things."

"They aren't impossible." Her arms were still crossed. I knew that she liked to read books about telepathic abilities and all. However, it was different when you were confronted with an example in real life, your life.

"That's what I'm trying to tell you. This *is* possible. He might disappear. If he does, then I'll decide if I want to find out more about what happened. If he doesn't, what am I supposed to do, crawl under a rock?"

She's acting like you should go to a hospital.

I'm afraid that's true, I responded.

"Is he talking to you now?" She uncrossed her arms and rubbed her hands.

"Are you cold?" I said and checked the thermostat. Whenever I left the condo or when I could snuggle underneath a couple of blankets, I turned the temperature down to seventy degrees out of habit. I pushed the electronic screen until the temperature read seventy-three.

"He's talking to you, isn't he?"

"He talked to me before I looked at the thermostat. He said you didn't believe us. He was the one that wanted to go to Dr. Randall's office the day after the murder."

She mouthed the word.

We were always together. As much as he annoyed me, Sherlock seemed more reticent than I would have expected, and he hadn't given any sign that he listened to me all the time.

"We're both conscious. When Sherlock takes over my body, I'm right there watching."

"Are you sure?"

Up until then, I hadn't been sure. "I am. He's a part of me."

She got up from her chair and felt my forehead. "You're not running a fever."

"Okay, ask him whatever you want." I was running out of ideas. "Ask him about his life." I didn't know that much about him myself. Maybe I was starting to believe he was real.

"I don't know anything about the Victorian era. That's when he lived, isn't it?"

"Yes, it is," Sherlock answered.

I wanted her to believe me, even if I was crazy. "Do you remember how I talked after Dr. Randall's murder?"

"You didn't recognize me," she said.

"I was talking about him."

"And he didn't know who you were?" El had an excellent memory.

She is beginning to understand.

Sherlock gently took control. "Before I awoke in Sissy's mind, I remembered being very old, hardly able to move. When I awoke, I had no physical manifestation at all until I discovered that I could live through her. It is quite exhilarating."

"If you are the same person with the same soul, shouldn't you merge?" El asked.

That shocked Sherlock to silence. Naturally, he would want to continue to exist as a separate entity.

"If there were any records of a similar situation, we might be able to answer that question. To our knowledge, we're the only case. I don't know if we'll merge," I answered for us both. It might have been easier if I'd just kept Sherlock's existence a secret. "I went to a psychiatrist over in Gaithersburg," I continued.

"What happened?"

I told her how Dr. Hessman thought I killed Dr. Randall before laughing me out of her office.

"I'm sure there are good psychiatrists around," she added.

I was mistaken. She does not believe I am real. If she did, she would not suggest that you go to another doctor.

"Sherlock thinks you're saying we should go to another doctor."

"No. But if you want to…"

I'd grown used to him like a person could grow used to a dog who chewed their shoes. "I'm not sure. I haven't given it much thought."

"It would be extraordinary," she said.

"But?"

"What if you need help?" El did look concerned. Her face had softened as she studied me.

I remembered this weird thing from when I was a kid. Something about how crazy people didn't think they're crazy and healthy people sometimes did.

"If other people pop up, I'll tell you, okay?"

"Okay."

Only time would convince us both of my sanity. Relieved that I'd finally told El about Sherlock, I took a deep breath.

El switched gears as mercurially as her Gemini birthdate predicted. "Should we go to the bank?"

"Do we have to?"

She laughed.

"I forgot that I do need to go to the store." I didn't want to run out of toilet paper. The gray skies outside reminded us that the weather had changed in Maryland over the past decade. Today, the temperature hovered around the freezing mark, ideal for a heavy wet snowfall if the Nor'easter storm coming up the east coast stalled over Maryland.

Chapter 21

Vehicles had swamped the *Stop and Go* store when I pulled in to get gas. El and I both agreed running out of gas during a snowstorm would be a bad call.

I saw a scraggly young man put a handwritten sign on the door that said sold out of bread and toilet paper in huge letters.

Expletive-deletive. It would take hours to shop at a supermarket.

"This Parker fellow works only a few blocks away from Dr. Randall's office. Isn't that odd?"

"What's that?" My mind kept drifting back to my toilet paper situation.

"All the people involved in the case seem to be located fairly close to one another. Marcus lived farther away just like you do. Williamson was his connection."

"Like a web."

Not many cars were on Wisconsin Avenue. Most places on the avenue that went all the way into Washington, D.C. didn't sell gas or toilet paper—at least not this close to the Beltway. El wanted to go to the bank. We didn't need to use the public parking lot since a space opened up in front of the big brick building.

"He might be gone," I said.

The bank—a ritzy kind of place—was open. The heavy brass door swung to the side on well-oiled hinges.

Chandeliers hung from the tall ceiling and the room appeared to stretch to most of the depth of the building.

We found Parker sitting in a row of identical desks, with a brass name plate I couldn't read until we stood directly in front of him. He looked very muscular under his nice suit as if he had played football in high school or college and visited the gym on a regular basis even now.

"What can I help you with today?" he said crisply.

"A Mr. Williamson said you went to school together," El said. The hushed atmosphere of the paneled walls and the crystal lights must have brought back her polite persona.

"Yes, many of us attended the same private high school, St. Barnabas. Do you know it? I enjoy going back to the school's functions." He seemed sincere and happy about his school.

"We're making a private inquiry into a delicate matter. Did you know Dr. Randall?" Parker's expression changed. He lowered his head. "The whole episode upset all of us," he whispered. "The shooting happened not far from here. A murder has never happened in Bethesda before—not to my knowledge at least."

He must not read the newspapers.

"Did you know her?" El whispered back.

"I told Williamson about her when he applied for a loan. She helped me quit smoking." Parker nodded. "I suppose I don't look like I would smoke. The coaches always wanted me to quit, but I couldn't until she hypnotized me."

"She helped me quit smoking too," I said.

"Then you understand how miraculous it was to stop so easily. I gained a few pounds and lost them after I started going to the gym again."

"You didn't have any trouble at all after your session with her?" I asked.

He looked at me oddly. "What for? She was a psychiatrist."

Parker might not have any deep dark secrets. If he didn't, he *might have* referred Williamson as a favor. "Did Mr. Williamson get his loan?"

"What sort of inquiry are you doing?" When I didn't answer, he continued, "Mr. Williamson probably told you I didn't give him the loan. He didn't have enough collateral."

"Your classmate has a lovely house, though." El was in her best schmoozing mode.

"He refused to put it up as collateral. Can't say that I blame him. You don't want to risk losing your house if you're not sure your venture will succeed. That's what convinced me that I couldn't approve his loan. If his house had been fully mortgaged, I might have considered approving the loan, for old time's sake."

I never understood before how the banks collapsed during the financial crisis. But if they all made decisions like Parker's, they wouldn't last long.

"You see," he said looking at me disapprovingly as though he could read my mind, "our alumni have a great track record. They pay their debts."

We weren't getting anything out of him, it seemed. So much for driving around before a snowstorm.

"Well, thank you for your time," El said.

Normally, the ride back to my place would only take about ten minutes unless we hit a snag on the Beltway. Today, everyone seemed to have things they wanted to get done before the storm.

"I can't see him on our list," El stated matter-of-factly.

We drove the rest of the way in silence. Once we'd arrived, El slipped out of the car. She said she'd go pick up some clean clothes, maybe even stop for ribs if our favorite barbecue place was still open. As I walked up to my building, I was deep in thought about my conversation with El about Sherlock.

"Can I talk to you?" I recognized the melodious voice of Detective Kirkland. He stepped out of the shadows near the entrance to my building.

"Do I have a choice?" I'd been looking forward to a little peace and quiet.

"I'll take that to be a yes." He held the door open and followed me.

I guess my wish wasn't going to be granted. "Take it any way you want."

We didn't talk again until we were inside my condo. I offered some coffee and brewed his first and enjoyed the fragrance as the coffeemaker filled his cup. "Is black okay?"

"Cream if you've got it." He'd taken a seat at the breakfast bar.

"What do you want to talk about?" I asked after I started the machine to brew a cup for myself. I handed him his coffee and the creamer I'd opened for El.

Kirkland poured in it into his coffee until it was very light, about the color of an Irish half and half. "Not what, who. I want to talk about Louise."

I cocked an eyebrow.

The wind blew up against the patio doors so hard, I glanced at the windows to see if they'd held. "Why don't we sit in the living room?" I lit the gas fire before sitting on the couch.

Kirkland chose Harry's chair which didn't surprise me. It looked like a man's chair.

"Don't tell me you haven't seen her face plastered all over the news."

"I hardly ever watch the news." It just wasn't part of my routine. I'd never been home early enough to watch the evening news when I worked. My habits didn't change that much after I retired. Last night, I'd only switched on the news to see if a snowstorm was coming.

"I'm not here to give you a hard time. I just want to talk." He looked as sincere as when he accused El of Dr. Randall's murder.

"Oh right. You're here as a friend." Expletive-deletive. I reminded myself not to swear out loud at a policeman. I clamped my mouth shut and stared at the patio doors after a gust of wind hit them again.

"Louise disappeared yesterday. Her father doesn't know where she is. Do you have anything to say about that?" Kirkland looked like he was getting mad again.

A ray of sunshine broke through the clouds. "No, there's nothing to say except…"

If you can't say anything positive, say nothing at all, Sherlock whispered in my head.

I'd been accepting Sherlock's existence, but I should have known better. He really had a way of pushing my buttons.

"Except, what?"

I took a deep breath. "Except what do you expect? That I hope she's found safe? Of course, I do."

"Has El remembered anything that her friend Marcus told her? What is the lobbyist's name?" He leaned forward.

"I don't know," I said, which was the absolute truth. I wondered if he'd found more in Marcus' file. "Wouldn't he have more reason to hurt Marcus and El than anyone else?

"I can't question anyone without a name. Does your friend know anything?"

"She might."

"What were you doing today?"

Should I tell him about Williamson? That didn't seem like a good idea, if only I could keep my mouth shut

"We were in a bank not far from Dr. Randall's office. El is refinancing her condo." I waited to see if my information would mean anything to him.

He sat in Harry's chair as if he belonged there, sipping his coffee.

"The loan officer was a Mr. Parker."

Kirkland put his cup down on the coaster. I'd spent years trying to get Harry to remember to use the coasters I scattered around the room.

"When he started talking about how nervous the employees in the bank were because of the shooting, I asked him if he meant Dr. Randall's murder."

Now Kirkland's face blazed red.

"Turns out she hypnotized him too. She helped him quit his smoking habit. Said it worked great. You know about him, don't you?"

"How many times have I told you to stop investigating her murder?"

"It's not me. El can't let it go."

"She has to stop. Where is she by the way?" he asked when he realized she hadn't followed us into the condo.

The ray of sun disappeared, and the skies darkened. I flipped on a couple of lights. The firelight alone was too intimate.

"Where did she go?" he demanded.

"She'll be back. We were together most of the day." I hoped she *was* okay.

"Everyone else is taking this seriously. Why won't you two? Do you want to be shot?"

He looked like he was actually worried about us.

Please do not hypothesize.

I'd forgotten that Sherlock might be listening.

"I tried to keep her here, really, I did. You don't know how stubborn she is. And if someone wanted to shoot her, they've had plenty of opportunities."

He frowned. "Maybe you're right."

"Everybody involved in the case knows that she's had plenty of time to tell you anything she might know."

He sighed and asked for a bit more coffee. Kirkland probably lived on the stuff. He looked tired. I went to the kitchen to fix us both another cup.

"You never told me where Louise is," he said as I returned.

"I don't know." If I'd known, I wouldn't have told him anyway. There was no need for them to drag her into this. It was bad enough that she'd lost her mother. Two people had died, and those left behind deserved a little consideration.

"Louise is an expert marksman."

El knocked before she opened the door and jumped a little at the sight of Kirkland sitting in my living room. He saw her and his demeanor changed entirely, his body stiffening into that of a perfectly poised detective.

"I'll leave you two to your dinner." He was gone before I could ask him how he found out that Louise was a marksman.

"What did he want?" El put a bag of food on the table.

The ribs smelled good. I hadn't realized I was so hungry.

"He wanted to make sure we were okay."

El laughed, making her look years younger. "He likes you."

I didn't answer. She didn't need to know she was still in danger, not tonight.

When I closed the drapes, the living room was cozy with the table lamps glowing and the flickering flames in the fireplace. I took the coffee cups over to the sink. "Why don't we drink wine with dinner?"

"Let me choose," El said.

We'd been touring all the wineries in Virginia and Maryland since we retired. I'd collected a few bottles that I'd tasted and liked. El's taste wasn't exactly the same as mine, but I let her pick from my collection all the same.

Kirkland hadn't been waiting for me because he liked me.

He still thinks she is a likely target.

The detective wouldn't have shown up at my door if Louise wasn't missing. Randall was protecting his daughter by sending her away. It was better that way. She wouldn't be safe until we discovered the identity of the murderer.

Day 11
Chapter 22

El was still sleeping.

If Harry had been alive, he would have told me to get out of his chair and tell me to stop investigating my hypnotist's murder.

Did you ever sit in his chair when he was alive?

Harry already had a favorite chair when I met him. Through the years, when it became too shabby, I'd always insisted that we shop for a new one—preferably something that wouldn't be too ugly. I couldn't remember any time when I'd sat in one of his chairs.

He might not have cared if you occasionally sat in his chair.

It didn't matter. Harry was gone and unlike Sherlock, probably for good. Even if he woke up in some other man, Harry was so reasonable, he wouldn't want to complicate either of our lives by visiting.

He may not have told you to stop investigating your hypnotist's murder either.

Maybe not.

My purpose was to keep El out of trouble. Her involvement in Marcus' problems was reason enough to investigate Dr. Randall's murder. I'd decided to help my friend even when I disagreed with her in order to keep her safe.

Are you not intrigued by the puzzle?

The feel of the leather of Harry's chair no longer brought back the day of his death. It only brought back good memories. I felt alive again.

I did want to find out who shot my hypnotist.

You are becoming your true self.

My life with Sherlock Holmes at my side was becoming more real to me every day. I even thought that I remembered skulking around London in one of his disguises.

Then we will continue our inquiries, Sherlock said.

Not so fast. If we were only talking about me, I would agree.

Miss El's desire to find Marcus' killer has not diminished.

The grandfather clock that had been in Harry's family for three generations chimed ten times. Since El was usually an early riser, I rushed to her room. And discovered her neatly made bed and a note on the pillow that read:

"I'm sorry that I dragged you into this mess. Please stay home. El."

I wanted to call her, but my cell phone wasn't in my purse, and I hadn't written down El's newest number anywhere else so, I couldn't call her on my landline phone that I hardly ever used. I finally found my cell phone underneath my bed along with a lot of other stuff that had gone missing.

"Where are u?" I texted when she didn't answer my phone call.

"U stay safe," she wrote back to me. She didn't answer any of my texts after that.

We must find her.

For once, I agreed with Sherlock that we needed to move quickly.

Outside the first snow drifted to earth in large clusters. The tops of the cars in the parking lot were already covered. I'd parked my car in the garage so I wouldn't have to dig it out this morning.

Where would El go first? She never struck me as a vain person even though she spent a lot of time making herself look good. Her own habits would dictate she'd first return home for makeup and a warmer coat and snow boots.

I needed to get dressed in multiple layers in case I got stuck anywhere. Luckily, my mismatched outfit didn't take long to put together because El already had a head start.

I felt terrible that she was by herself in a world where people we knew were getting shot. I had to find her.

Chapter 23

The first snowfall of the year transformed the roads into white tunnels. Snow was already piled up on either side of the road and the steady snowfall had turned the air above us into a ceiling of sorts. I drove slower and slower because the visibility had become so bad. When I approached the traffic lights, all I could see were muted spots of amber, red, or green.

First snows were supposed to be light, giving the graying mid-Atlantic landscape a fresh look. This looked more like a blizzard though the news report hadn't predicted a heavy storm last night. The old saying of wait fifteen minutes if you want the Maryland weather to change popped into my head. I would have turned on the news if I didn't have to give all my attention to the road. After slowing down, I could see far enough through the thick white snow to stop safely at a red light.

A car in front of me fishtailed as the traffic light turned green. I waited for them to straighten out and move several car lengths forward before I took my foot off the brake.

The six blocks to El's condo took forever. Was it too much to wish she stayed home?

Perhaps not, Sherlock chimed in, *you know her very well.*

I sat with the motor running outside, thinking about what he said. At work, El had been methodical—not unusual for someone who studied the hard sciences and evaluated the scientific method of others clinical trials day in and day out.

She would've gone over the list of suspects we'd been interviewing and visit them again to see if she could get the same or more information. Or she might've drilled down further, looking to answer the questions that could lead us to the killer.

Would she focus more on Marcus' death than on the murder? If the same person killed both her former lover and my doctor, well, that wouldn't be a problem.

El had never told me who the lobbyist was. There might be other things she didn't know I thought as I pulled into the parking lot at her condo.

I figured she'd left shortly before I went into my living room. She'd probably had more than enough time to leave before the snow started. When I left my building, the layer of snow on the evergreens was at least an inch deep. At the rate it had been snowing, she'd been gone a half-hour before I discovered her note. She had probably left her condo by now.

First, you must check to make sure she is not here.

I texted El that I'd parked outside her building.

"Go home," she texted back.

She wasn't in. Where would she have gone? Yesterday, we'd discovered the identity of the young blond woman before we'd gone to visit Williamson.

Mr. Randall said that we should come back tomorrow, remember?

Sherlock was better than one of those daily organizers that I kept in my purse and didn't use. Maybe he could remember emails, phone numbers, and addresses too. I snorted.

Are we not in a hurry?

I tried to explain to Sherlock that the fastest way to go to Mr. Randall's house was to take the Beltway. The highway would probably be the safest route too after the snowplows spewed out their salt. We wouldn't be able to go too fast even if the road had been cleared. The ramp appeared on the right. I took the initiative and pulled onto the highway.

I would have to hurry if I expected to find El at Randall's house. I would have called if I'd had his phone number with me. El had been the one to write it down.

The short drive took over forty-five minutes. A fender bender on the Beltway blocked traffic in the right-hand lane for a while, messing up the other lanes as drivers moved away from the accident. If I tried to change lanes, I had no idea if I could accelerate quickly enough to blend into the flow of traffic. All the time, I kept thinking about El. She was so stubborn.

We hadn't talked much about Randall after we'd found out about his daughter. If I was interviewing him, what would I ask? A space opened up in the traffic before I could figure it out. I had to concentrate on staying out of the way of the other drivers who flew down the road as if nothing could ever happen to them.

Relief filled me when I finally came to the ramp for Connecticut Avenue.

I spent at least another ten minutes finding his house before pulling into a clear parking spot in his driveway. Judging by the tracks in the snow, someone had recently parked there.

El is not here.

The only positive thought I had was that nothing had happened to her since she'd been able to drive her car when she left. Sherlock didn't agree this was a good sign.

We must talk to Mr. Randall.

My wishful thinking was getting in the way of common sense. Mr. Randall didn't take long to answer the door.

"Have you seen my friend, El?"

"Come back to the kitchen. There's coffee and muffins."

I repeated my question as he poured me a cup of black coffee.

Calm concern had replaced the tortured grief I'd recognized during my last visit. He held out a basket filled with huge muffins marked by succulent-looking blue-purple spots. "Blueberry. They're delicious. Your friend brought them."

"Why didn't you answer my question?"

"She told me to not tell you anything," Randal said putting down the basket. "But I already slipped up and told you she brought the muffins."

I snorted.

"I don't mean to be difficult. She was adamant." He could have been a decent sort I supposed, and easy-going enough to be swayed by a strong-minded female.

Someone like his wife who liked pink so much.

Only a slight hum from the refrigerator and the wind blowing outside interrupted the silence inside the house. Snow caught at the corners of the window that framed the darkening scene outside. The street lamps flickered on and created rose-colored spots in the white landscape.

"Is your daughter home?"

Mr. Randall frowned. "Why do you want to know?"

First, he lost his wife, and then Randall would lose his daughter if Kirkland arrested her. He would protect her as well as he could.

"The house is quiet."

"Sorry. I thought you might be adding her to your list of suspects." He propped his head in two hands, leaning on the table. "She's never had any idea what her mother did except for the professional duties."

"Her grief seemed real enough to me." I took a sip of coffee. "Detective Kirkland did say that she's an expert marksman."

"He asked her where she was when Phillipa died." Randall's eyes filled with tears as he lifted his head. "Louise loved her mother very much."

We'd kept Randall on the top of our list, and Kirkland had probably done the same. Both the father and daughter would automatically have motives.

"And you?" I asked. Even as the words came out of my mouth, I realized my words sounded more like a statement than a question.

"I can see you understand how difficult it is to lose someone like a spouse." He gazed down at his hands.

"What did El say?" I swiftly moved past our shared discomfort. "What did El say?"

A tear slid down his cheek that he quickly brushed away. "She asked about Louise like you did. I told her that I'd sent her over to Columbia to stay with a friend."

"As long as she can prove where she was that day, she'll be fine."

"You think you know who killed my wife." Dark circles under his eyes made him look a little creepy.

"I *have* eliminated you from my list."

"After I talked to her about Louise, your friend decided that she didn't need to find her. She said she agreed with something the detective had said."

I couldn't remember her saying anything about Kirkland to me.

"He wanted to know the names of all the people who'd been blackmailed. He asked me to go over Phillipa's books and identify the large deposits made since we moved to Maryland. I gave the bank authorization to release all the information to him. He didn't really need that from me, but he said that should be enough to keep his superiors from charging me too." Randall looked at me mournfully, his bushy red eyebrows forming a peak in the center of his forehead.

With Dr. Randall dead and her husband in the clear, restitution could be made to the blackmail victims. I assumed the whole scheme could stay out of the papers. If I had a child, I wouldn't want her to live with the world knowing her mother had been blackmailing her patients. I had a feeling it would have hurt Randall's business too. Accountants had to operate under ethical standards.

"It's selfish of me to want to make the blackmailing go away. My family's reputation means more to me than catching the killer. Philippa," Randall's voice broke, "she's paid dearly for her greediness."

"She didn't match my idea of a blackmailer."

"I was surprised when I found out too. We didn't need the money." The man blew his nose loudly. Although it abruptly broke the silence in the house, it was a welcome sound.

"You have no idea where El went?" I asked and glanced outside once more. I could barely see across the street.

"Is she in danger? She told me that her friend Marcus had been killed."

The snow had imbedded itself in the screen and completely covered the lower half of the window.

"I better go." I walked into the front room past the cheerful fire that made all the pink colors in the living room look golden. I slipped my feet into my wet tennis shoes. Why did I wear tennis shoes when I had perfectly good boots in the closet? That was a mystery I didn't think I would ever solve, even with Sherlock's help.

"You might try that Rudy character. She seemed to be worried about him. That other one, Mr. Williamson, she didn't seem to care what might happen to him. I think she felt a little guilty about leaving Rudy to his own devices." He helped me into my coat.

"I know your wife blackmailed Rudy, Marcus, and Williamson. How many others were there?"

Randall looked away.

"If you tell me, it will help me protect my friend."

Kirkland would never tell me about the blackmail victims even if he did think one of them was the murderer. For all we knew, someone we would never suspect, someone with a different motive could be the killer.

"I wouldn't want anything to happen to your friend." Randall wrapped his arms around his body. "I'm not sure that you should be going out in this weather."

A plow had made its way past the house already leaving a dirty pile of snow behind my car. "If I stay here much longer, I'll have no choice."

He opened the main door leaving me to struggle with the storm door myself. I trudged back to my car, taking giant steps to clear the top of the snow when Randall called out to me.

"Four, that I know of."

"Who was the fourth?" I yelled.

He shook his head.

"The fourth?" I yelled again hoping that I wouldn't have to walk back to the door.

"Welker," he yelled back. From the look on his face, he hadn't been happy to find out about the last victim, the same man who had scared me the most of all the people we'd interviewed.

The doctor's anger had seemed irrational. Being a blackmail victim and fearing he might lose his business to her too, might have made him even more dangerous.

My car started right up, and I floored it after I put it in reverse.

No swear words? Sherlock asked.

I ignored him and set the heat up as far as it would go. The situation might yet call for my extended vocabulary. Headlights, windshield wipers, heat—I'd turned on all the essential functions even though we only had a few blocks to drive to Rudy's house.

What little sunlight that had been darting through spaces between the clouds quickly dimmed. Only the street lights lit the road now. Up ahead, I could see the red lights of a large vehicle that I assumed would be a plow.

It turned out to be a garbage truck of all things. I stopped, left my car running, and went to see what the problem was.

"We blockin' your way?" a grizzled man yelled out. He wore one of those red and black checkered hats with the ear flaps that I thought only existed in the movies.

"Are you alright?" I didn't know what I would be able to do for this character that he couldn't do for himself.

"That's what I should be asking you," he laughed as he twirled the silver wrench around one more time on a huge bolt that appeared to be part of the apparatus holding a plow to the front of the truck.

"You best get yourself going to wherever you should be. There's room enough for you to drive around my truck."

Thank goodness, another car had already made tread marks through the snow. My car wouldn't have to push the snow aside, but the tread marks might be slippery.

"Looks like I'm good to go. Good luck to you," I said and jumped back in my car. Those few minutes outside had turned my feet to ice.

He waved after I successfully passed him. Only a minute later, I could barely see the two smudges of light made by the truck's headlights

El would always be one step ahead of me. When I saw the distinctive dark cross beams against the white plaster ahead, it only took me a moment to remember Rudy had been staying with his mom since Marcus' murder.

No tire tracks marked his driveway either. Unless El parked on the street, she hadn't made the same mistake.

I was never going to find her.

Perhaps you should let her find you. She may already be home, Sherlock said.

Even with the defroster blasting away, only small circles of the windows and windshield were clear. I was an idiot. No one would be out trying to take a pot shot at El in this storm. Of course, neither one of us, not even the weatherman, had known it would snow so much, so fast. An Irish Jig from my phone interrupted my thoughts.

It was El. "You'll never believe what Mr. Randall told me."

"That Dr. Randall blackmailed Welker too?"

"So, you visited him? Why didn't you stay home?"

I didn't reply.

"No wonder his office had seen better days. I'm going to pay him a visit," El said after a moment.

At least she'd called me.

My car suddenly darkened. While I'd been talking to El, a thick layer of snow had covered my windshield again. My defrost was losing its battle against the fog covering the inside too. I rubbed the inside with some paper towels I'd left in the car for something or other and turned on the windshield wipers again.

"Can't we go tomorrow?"

"I'm sitting in front of his house now."

"How did you find his address?"

"I called his office line and got his service. They gave me his phone number. He said he wouldn't mind talking to me once I told him about Marcus."

When I told her where I was, she said I was only about six blocks away. Much to my dismay, I realized I would have to navigate the warren of streets to get there.

"Just get back on Wisconsin and drive down to Walsh if you want to meet me. That should be easier. At least Wisconsin is clear."

"I'll see you at my place," I said, hanging up. I'd had enough of chasing around after El for one day. What had I been thinking?

Clumps of snowflakes continued falling, dimming the brightness of the traffic lights ahead on Wisconsin Avenue. The street was plowed and not all that slippery, though snow mountains covered the sidewalks. Snowplows had cleared the Beltway by the time I made it there, leaving only a little slush on the two open lanes. Most of the traffic I'd seen earlier had disappeared. The going was harder in Silver Spring close to my condo, but I eventually pulled into my garage, glad there were no witnesses to see my sorry state.

There was just enough time for me to slip out of my wet clothes and shoes into pajamas and slippers before El arrived. She didn't look much better than I did.

She hadn't gone to visit Rudy at all after seeing Randall. Once she found out that Dr. Welker had also been blackmailed, El had made a beeline to his house.

"It was fine, really."

I was still a little mad at her from not telling me the truth, now anger surged through me again. "There was no way for you to know that it was safe. Dorothy wasn't even there to protect you."

"Do you want to know what happened?"

I wasn't sure that I did.

"He admitted that he'd been blackmailed."

Kirkland already knew that Welker was the fourth blackmail victim. El had risked her life for nothing.

"If you're not interested, I'll go home."

I didn't stop her from leaving. It was no good trying. I couldn't keep her safe.

Day 12
Chapter 24

My phone danced a jig on my bedside table.

Why don't you talk to her? Sherlock said.

I wanted to sleep. The clock beside my bed said 7:00 in large red numbers. The sound stopped and started up again before I finally answered my phone.

"What about the snow? Can't I stay in bed today?" I said to El. Since Dr. Randall died, I'd been sleeping every night. The more sleep I had, the more I wanted.

Instead of dreaming about Harry, I dreamt about the two little rat boys from the pictures in Dr. Randall's office. They had stolen the mayor's watch in one of the pictures. Sometimes I saw them peeking in the window at Mr. Tessmeyer's house. Other times, they were sneaking around Dr. Welker's desk, always with a sarcastic look—one corner of their mouths pulled up, wide eyes as if they were making fun of us.

"I'm not sure that it's healthy for you to sleep so much. Have you been drinking your coffee in the morning?" El asked.

I nodded and remembered she couldn't see me. "Yep. At least I'm sleeping through the night." When I was a kid, even when I came home from college for the holidays, Aunt Pet always said that I must need sleep when I wanted to sleep till noon.

"That's true." El agreed. "Jessica wants to meet us. The roads are clear, and the snow is already melting. Why don't we meet at the Pit?"

"You're not going to meet her early, are you?"

She paused. "I'll call her back and tell her I can't meet her until 11:00. You can meet us there at 11:30." In the background, I could hear El tapping the stylus for her tablet. I wasn't the only one with nervous habits. She often did this whenever she was on the phone.

"Okay." I reached for the clock and pulled it to me so I could set my alarm for 10:45 just in case I did go back to sleep.

My phone buzzed and my clock radio blared out an Incubus song with a title I couldn't remember. I wondered if someone had slipped me a narcotic along the way.

"Yes," I shouted into my phone.

"It's 11:30, and you aren't here."

"Is Jessica there?" If she wasn't, I figured I could tell El to go ahead and eat without me.

"Yes." El's voice was louder. The restaurant must be busy today. I could hear plates scraping across tabletops, a waitress talking, and even a phone beeping out the song *Roll Out the Barrel*. "Come right away," she said.

"I'll be there in half an hour."

The angle of the sun through my bedroom window confirmed it was getting close to noon. I brushed my teeth, did that quick hair thing I sometimes do with a damp brush to make it look like I had at least tried to arrange my hair, and pulled on a striped black and white shirt with 'I'm old, not dead' written in red letters across my chest. El always laughed when she saw it. I hoped it would be enough to reduce her irritation with me. I had no idea why I was worried about her feelings after she had me chasing her yesterday,

Parking was a nightmare even though most of the snow had been cleared off Wisconsin Avenue. I finally parked four blocks away in a garage.

Walking was a good idea after staying in bed for so long. The bad disc in my back almost felt like it was going to slip out as I left my condo. Sometimes, it was better to keep moving and let it gradually ease into place. By the time I reached the restaurant, I was in good form.

I smiled at the two trim ladies who were waiting for me up a couple of stairs in the same curved booth we'd occupied when we first met Jessica. El didn't laugh when she saw my shirt. Jessica studied it for a moment and looked away.

"Sorry I'm late." If only I had a dollar for every time that I'd said that in my life. My fifteen-minute rule did not apply today since I should have been there at 11:30. My red watch now said 12:14.

Jessica raised her eyebrows and shrugged. "Don't worry about it. Not like I have anything on this afternoon."

El frowned. "I forgot that you don't have a job yet. I'm sorry."

"I told you I was fine, and that's true." She stared at her drink as if there was some answer there. Maybe she was mad at me for being late.

I checked to see if that boyfriend of hers had popped the question as Jessica reached for her ice tea. There wasn't any flashy diamond on the ring finger of her left hand. In fact, she didn't look as perky as she had when we met her. She was wearing a drab gray shirt that had seen better days, and black pants that could have been bought at a uniform store.

"Did you move in with your boyfriend?" I hoped that was a happy topic for her.

"Not yet. We're still looking at condos."

The boyfriend wasn't so great after all.

"Did you order?" I hoped that El had gone ahead and ordered a salad for me, but she shook her head.

"We waited for you." El fussed with her silverware, and Jessica looked down at her napkin.

El hadn't been herself ever since she had admitted her old boyfriend Marcus was being blackmailed by my hypnotist. I took this as a good sign—at least she felt guilty. El had other things to worry about too, like losing her retirement pension. That's what had gotten us into this mess. If anything happened to my retirement, I would still be in good shape. Not so for most people.

Harry had been a planner, but El didn't have a dead husband. Her retirement could still be on the line if our agency figured out that she'd breached the rules of conduct.

I missed the old El.

She crooked her finger at the waitress. My friend was still there, getting her own way. I hoped that in time I would be able to get past our problems.

I ordered my favorite chicken salad and a Diet Coke. The caffeine would help.

One thing was painfully clear after we mulled over the facts of the case. Dr. Randall's office had too many doors. Patients entered through the front door into the waiting room. The only other door went into the treatment area with the pink chairs which in turn, had a door going into the doctor's personal office.

While Jessica could see the patients in the waiting room through the two-way mirror, there was no door from the waiting room into her office. The only door into the receptionist's area opened into Dr. Randall's personal office. That meant that there were three doors into the doctor's office: the one from the treatment area, the one from the receptionist's office, and the back door. The killer could have easily slipped in from the hall without being seen.

Please ask the young lady why she called Miss El.

I'd almost forgotten Sherlock was there. He might have been upset about our wild goose chase yesterday. If he had thought it was a bad idea to hunt for El, he should have said something before we left the condo.

El put us back on track before I could ask.

"Jessica said that she thought she might have figured out why you couldn't remember much from your session with Dr. Randall." She spoke loud enough for me to hear her above all the noise in the restaurant.

"It's the hypnotism. You could have had trouble coming out of the hypnotic trance because Dr. Randall said she would tell you when your session was over."

"If someone," Jessica said. I thought she meant the person who'd killed Dr. Randall. "Told you not to remember their faces and go to sleep until the end of the hour, that would explain what happened too."

El's eyebrows shot up. "They could have made us do anything?"

"Not quite. People have limits." Jessica looked down at her napkin again. She might be remembering a suggestion that the not-so-good doctor had tried on her.

Do not even consider...

I was sure he was going to say that he was not the result of a hypnotic suggestion. The idea made me smile. There might be an easy way out of my personal dilemma.

It won't work.

"Is he speaking to you now?" El frowned.

Jessica looked confused. "What's going on?"

"Nothing for you to worry about."

El wasn't appeased. "You didn't answer me."

The talking, the clattering of dishes and silverware, even the rushing of traffic outside, seemed to have diminished as if the people at other tables were listening. Even a girl with blond hair pulled back in a bun cleaning the front doors had stopped wiping the glass.

"Later," was all I said.

El raised one eyebrow before looking at Jessica. "Thanks. The problem is that we don't know enough to make much sense of all this."

"I'm not so worried about understanding hypnotism," I said.

That much was true. Sherlock was a different problem.

Then you do believe I exist.

El crinkled her nose as if she was catching on.

"Who would know that they could implant a suggestion?" I didn't want to think that it was Mr. Randall. For some reason that I didn't understand, I needed to protect him.

He has a daughter.

Sherlock was right. Mr. Randall's daughter had acted like she could have predicted the next word that would come out of her father's mouth. It didn't matter that Dr. Randall had blackmailed her patients. Both husband and daughter were clearly devastated by her murder and were very close.

Jessica shook her head. "I don't know. Hypnotism can be tricky. It's hard to know if an amateur could've pulled it off. The killer probably thought it was worth a shot."

The waitress came with the bill.

"I guess that's our cue to leave," El said. She grabbed the check as I reached forward. "My treat."

I gave her a look.

"No arguments now." El smiled.

"Okay."

El pulled out her card, and the waitress was immediately there to take it. My friend already had on her coat, so I dragged on my denim jacket.

"Thanks for lunch." Jessica was hanging back as if planning to leave the restaurant with us. She'd said that she wasn't in a rush. If I was her age, I wouldn't have been hanging around with two old ladies. Didn't she have any friends her own age?

I glanced over at El wondering if she had any idea what I'd been thinking. She wouldn't like me calling her an old lady. From a distance, a passerby would probably take decades off El's true age. Only up close could you see the wrinkles at the corners of her eyes.

The glass doors gleamed with a greenish tinge, making the street look slightly ill.

Jessica grabbed the handle of the door. The room behind us hushed as if everyone in the restaurant was watching us leave. Did they know we were involved in a murder investigation?

El looked up and smiled. She stepped forward beside Jessica, her black hair flying back as the cooler air from outside rushed through the door.

I turned as the bullet hit her. A dark spot bloomed on her shoulder, inches away from Jessica. Glass broke behind us. A waitress held on to the handle of the broken mug for a moment before she let it crash to the floor.

El's mouth opened in an "O," and she went down.

Quick, Sissy, Sherlock prompted me.

I knelt by my friend. She wasn't unconscious, although I was sure she was stunned by what had happened. As I bit back a sob, I realized she was talking to me.

"I'll call 911," El said struggling to get her phone out of her purse. "Get back," she said, looking at the street. "/The shooter might still be here."

She wanted me to move away from the door. If Sherlock had been standing beside me, I'm sure he would have been shaking his head. El was my best friend. I would do anything for her. There was no way I could desert her.

You have to try and catch the shooter or at least identify them, Sherlock said and took control.

No one was on the sidewalk on either side of the street in front of the restaurant. They must have run after the shot.

Focus, he said as we moved in front of El, shielding her with my body.

Off to the right, a grayed-hair man ran down the block with a boy in tow. If the person who'd fired the shots was a psycho, I thought, he should be shooting them right now.

If that means the shooter does not care who he kills, I agree. Stay low.

An older, broad-bumpered mustard-colored Mercedes was parked in front of a white BMW that screeched away from the curb after a man suddenly appeared behind the wheel. The older man and boy had disappeared. Traffic had stopped going west on Wisconsin Avenue. A blue Camry roared past going east.

No one was on the sidewalk close to me except El and Jessica.

The shooter must be across the street, Sherlock said.

I heard another thud and a scream. There was something wet on my cheek.

Now! Behind the car.

I hesitated. Sherlock took control and ran.

In front, a one-story blue building facing the restaurant had a red and blue FedEx sign on its flat roof. A part of the building appeared to be divided into a separate retail space with a For Lease sign above the door. Light glared off of something metallic beside the frame supporting the sign on the roof.

We need to cross the street.

I didn't want to go out in the open. For a moment, I knew it was very possible that if I stood up again, I would be shot.

Sirens wailed from both directions. Cop cars with flashing lights blocked off the street only a few seconds before a big black van arrived.

An officer wearing a black bullet-proof vest appeared by my side and helped me to my feet.

I pointed up to the roof. The flash of sunlight off something metal had disappeared. "There was someone there, but they're gone."

Detective Kirkland crouched as he loped his way down the street toward me.

"I'm pretty sure the shot came from the roof," I said after he arrived. I thought he would be worried about capturing the shooter.

"Are you insane?" he grabbed me roughly by the arms before he realized what he'd done. He let go and stepped back.

"Don't you want to catch the shooter?" The words tumbled out of my mouth before I had a chance to think about what I was saying.

He took a deep breath before he spoke. "Did you see who it was?" he demanded.

I didn't have a chance to answer. Two men, also dressed in black vests and helmets with clear visors, stopped abruptly in the middle of the street when they saw us. One of the men lifted his visor and motioned to Kirkland to join him. The street was still blocked off.

While he was otherwise occupied, I went back to the newly-arrived ambulance where El was being loaded on a gurney. She wasn't happy about being manhandled.

"At least let me sit up," I heard her say.

One of the EMTs leapt forward.

"Make her come with us," El said pointing at me and still struggling against the strap that held her on the gurney.

Sherlock wasn't having any of it. "We're not going anywhere."

Suddenly, Kirkland was at our side. "What's going on?"

"Why aren't you searching for the shooter?" Sherlock said. He was in control and angry. Maybe he was more affected by what I felt than I thought.

"Why don't you go with your friend? We'll take care of this." Kirkland said.

He took my arm.

That was the worst thing that he could have done.

Anger surged through our body. I wanted to warn Kirkland that he should duck, but my mouth wasn't under my control either

Our fist flew through the air. I saw the surprise on Kirkland's face, heard the scream that came from El, before my fist connected with the detective's chin. There was a distinctive crack.

It didn't come from Kirkland.

The physical pain was the worst that I'd felt in a long time. Yet Sherlock wasn't done.

El yelled again. "Stop, Sherlock!"

He wasn't thinking. I suppose he was reacting physically to the pain and his anger. All this was going through my head as we tackled Kirkland.

Two uniforms pulled us off the stunned detective.

"Let go of me, you buffoons." Sherlock tried to pull away. The tactics he employed would have worked during his own era, especially if you considered that he was an athletic man or that was the way he remembered himself.

"Sissy, stop it," Kirkland said. He was on his feet a foot away from me.

"No," Sherlock said.

Kirkland backed away. "What do you mean?"

"You heard her," we said and pointed at El. "I'm Holmes." If I'd been in control of my body, I would have been shuddering.

"Sherlock Holmes?" one of the officers said, puzzled by my behavior

"Indeed. No other."

Kirkland tried to tell the men that we'd been kidding, but we'd hurt more pride than brawn.

I felt a prick in my arm and knew no more.

Day 13
Chapter 25

My hand was stuck in a vice. Dr. Welker twirled the bar controlling it, making it bear down on my hand. Except now, it wasn't Dr. Welker, but Harry. I tried to move my hand.

"Should I sedate her again?" a gruff female voice asked

My head wasn't working right. My body wasn't connected to my head.

Then I remembered that Harry had died over two years ago. He hadn't been holding the vice. He wouldn't be coming to rescue me from this place, whatever it was. Expletive-deletive!

My hand throbbed with every beat of my heart.

"She needs to get up and move around. I don't want fluid to collect in her lungs."

Ahh, we must not be severely injured.

I had heard that voice before. But my head refused to clear. A block of fog had attached itself to my conscious thought. Who was that?

Sherlock, of course.

Sherlock, as in Sherlock Holmes?

Yes, Sissy. You are my reincarnation, remember?

Impossible! Reincarnation was impossible. We live, we die. Period.

You're wrong. Just wait until you remember me.

Smoking. I'd wanted to quit smoking.

Someone murdered poor Dr. Randall in the light.

"The officers reported she'd been quite violent," The female voice said.

I remembered now. Sherlock had become so angry he'd lashed out at my detective. I guess he'd demonstrated that even an older woman can be dangerous if she's angry enough.

"She's pretty old to be causing much trouble. Her hand is broken in five places," the male voice said.

Pretty freaky being so discombobulated. Maybe this place was a dream. I don't think I like being in limbo.

That is how I feel until I take control of your body.

Why were we two separate entities?

Soon you'll remember that we tried to figure that out without success. I do hope that we don't merge any time soon. Wouldn't you miss me?

I shrugged mentally. Sherlock's presence seemed logical enough. He almost sounded like my internal voice of reason, the one saying what I imagined Harry would have said if he caught me acting before I thought things through.

"Let's wake her up," the male voice said.

I did like that voice. He sounded like he wanted to help me. Still, I had trouble thinking of anything but my throbbing hand.

"Can you open your eyes?"

I blinked. The lights shone brightly, reflecting off the white walls. I was right in the middle of the room, just as I'd been right in the middle of all that had happened since I went to the hypnotist.

"Do you know where you are?"

We have been confined.

"I must be in a hospital. My hand hurts." Straps held me down not letting me move. One pressured my hand. "Why am I strapped down?"

"Don't you remember what happened? the man said.

When I looked to my right, I could see the young man who sounded so nice.

"Someone shot my friend."

"The report says you punched a detective." A stethoscope hung around his neck. The nice man must be my doctor.

I imagine that I would be the subject of a good story he'd tell his wife about the old woman accused of attacking a policeman. A look into his eyes made me reassess him.

"Did you do that—I mean punch a cop?" He didn't seem to believe the report that I'd been violent. He wanted to know what might drive me to punch a man.

This is my fault, Sherlock said.

No kidding.

I needed to get out of here and see El.

"I did," I admitted. "They stopped looking for the person who shot my friend. Two other people have died. Is El okay?"

"I don't know," he said suddenly serious. "Was she brought in at the same time?"

"I think so. They'd already loaded her into the ambulance when someone gave me a shot."

The nurse stood beside the doctor holding a needle.

"I don't need more sedatives," I told him.

He waved the nurse away. "We don't need this. Two others. You must be talking about the psychiatrist and the other man shot in a parking garage."

The strap across my chest was gone, and the one across my legs fell away. I almost cried in relief when he loosened the strap holding down my right hand. For a moment, blood flooded into my damaged hand.

"That strap was far too tight, nurse," the doctor said and frowned.

She didn't blink.

"We aren't here to punish our patients." He reached over to take the blood pressure sleeve from a silver rack screwed into the wall.

"We certainly aren't here to coddle them either," she mumbled under her breath.

I liked this nurse less and less.

My hand demanded my attention. When I lifted it to my face, a green wrapping with some sort of splint covered most of it keeping my fingers stretched out flat. I tried to wiggle my ring finger.

"Don't try to move your fingers. Two of them are broken and the middle one needs some surgical work." He cradled my hand in his own and laid it down on my chest. "You must have been pretty mad."

"Yes, mad," the nurse said.

I'd talked myself out of worse predicaments. "It was such a shock. My best friend gunned down right in front of me. So much blood. I understand why crime victims often blame the police. It seemed like they should have been able to capture whoever shot at us." I put my hand to my head. "And a bullet hit me too, if I remember correctly. Everything happened so fast." My left hand found a bandage on my right temple.

"A bullet did graze your head. Nothing to worry about." The doctor took the blood pressure sleeve off my arm. "Your blood pressure is normal now. Do you take medication?"

"I don't. Do you think I should?" Being the respectful patient now was easy. "I'm sorry, I didn't catch your name."

"Dr. Arnold." He wrote a lot on that clipboard of his. "Your blood pressure was high when they brought you in. I will give you some medication for your hand, but there is this other matter of what you said. Who are you?" The doctor's face looked troubled. He was too young to have the deep creases that marked the old physicians I'd seen lately. He was looking for signs that I was nuts. If Sherlock had chosen that moment to talk to me, the doctor would have seen the change.

"I'm Sissy Holmes," I said as distinctly as I could. Sticking to my story.

He smiled. "Not Sherlock Holmes?"

"Heavens no. That would be ridiculous." I probably looked like hell, but I tried to smile sweetly.

"The officers said you insisted you were Sherlock Holmes."

"I do have a habit of saying, no blank Sherlock. I swear too much." I grimaced. "I suppose they could have misheard me. My last name is Holmes," I added.

"Your driver's license says Carpenter."

All I had to do was tell the truth now. "That's my married name. I lost my husband a few years ago."

"And your maiden name is Holmes?"

The doctor wanted to believe that this retired lady wasn't cuckoo. The fact that I was involved in a multiple murder case probably didn't help.

"Yes. I recently started going by my maiden name again. I've been planning on doing that for some time." Sticking to the truth always made it easier to lull others into acceptance.

"And why is that?"

I didn't want to go into too much detail. But he looked like he wanted to give me a break, so I decided that I would tell him whatever he wanted. "I was very depressed after my husband passed away. My friend—the one who was shot— has been wonderful. I don't know what I would do if I lost her.

These last few months, I've been trying to do everything I could to make myself whole again."

"This includes changing your name back to Holmes?"

"Yes. I do feel much better going by it. I still have to do all the paperwork." That was true. I wasn't Mrs. Carpenter any more—I was Sissy Holmes.

"These policemen jumped to the wrong conclusion," he said to the nurse. He handed her the clipboard. "We will have to keep you overnight, I'm afraid. That's hospital protocol."

"Shall I sedate her now?" the nurse asked picking up the syringe.

Dr. Arnold gave her a look. He scribbled something on a pad. "The only medication she needs is this," he said and handed the paper to the thin, but sturdy looking woman. I wouldn't be surprised if she worked at a job less stressful on a regular basis, if not for protection from crazy people, at least to help her nerves.

"What is it?" I asked.

"Something for the pain." He motioned to my hand. "The less you move it the better."

I would follow his instructions to the letter.

"Is it okay for me to stand up? My back is killing me." When my hand stopped hurting so much, my back would start complaining.

"A little exercise would do you good." Dr. Arnold motioned to the nurse. "Walk her down to her room."

I was sorry to see him go, but when you're lying, less is more.

After he was gone, the nurse helped me up.

"You weren't telling him the truth," she said.

I could have protested my innocence. Instead, I silently let her lead me down the shiny hallway to a door that looked like it belonged in a prison. A bruise was starting to darken on her left cheek. Maybe I'd hit her too when they brought me inside. The door and surrounding jam were painted the same color as the wall—a light green that reminded me of the psychiatrist in Gaithersburg, a calming color that was still an impenetrable metal barrier.

Claustrophobia wasn't one of my weaknesses. If it was, I would have been in trouble because the room had no window and was pretty small. The nurse held my arm until I safely sat down on the narrow bed attached to the wall.

"I'll be back with the pain killer." She accidentally, at least I hoped it was accidental, flicked her finger at my hand— not much, only enough to send pains shooting up my arm. Maybe she hated her job. I'd been lucky. Working at the FDA had been interesting most of the time.

I tried to hold back my tears. One escaped down my cheek.

Focus on something else.

I couldn't think about much. The pain overwhelmed me.

Who killed your hypnotist?

I'd spent over a week trying to figure that out. There were so many suspects, so many unforeseen circumstances. When I'd woken up in that room full of policemen, I had no idea that Dr. Randall had blackmailed her patients.

You didn't know that you were my reincarnation either.

I didn't know that El was still in love with Marcus.

And you didn't know that she broke up with him because he wouldn't stop using drugs.

When Sherlock said it like that, I felt even worse. Marcus had finally done what El wanted and would never get a chance to get her back. I was sure that she still loved him.

We didn't know that Dr. Randall agreed to stop blackmailing her patients.

Mr. Randall could have been lying.

You didn't think he was lying before.

Why did Rudy Tessmeyer go in to pay Dr. Randall off when she'd told her husband she would stop? Randall didn't say she agreed to stop. It sounded like something that happened in the past.

We have to get out of here.

The nurse finally came back with a couple of pills which I swallowed gratefully.

"Don't be surprised if Dr. Arnold changes his mind," she said.

"What do you mean?" I'd been focusing on the case like Sherlock wanted. When she'd entered the room, I lost my concentration and the pain rushed through me.

"If I write a bad report for you, he'll keep you in longer." Her harsh smile and those dark impenetrable eyes bore into me. She deserved to be called worse things than nasty. Maybe she was like this all the time. I didn't care if she hated her job.

A beat passed, and then, "I checked on your friend. She's in critical condition."

The shadowed room rotated around me.

Impossible. She had only been shot in the shoulder.

I replayed the scene in my mind. She'd been shot once, then I had put myself between her and the door. The next shot had gone high. I'd been standing when it grazed me.

"You are so gullible. Did you really think that I would go to all that trouble to find out about your friend? You can wait." The nurse bumped into my hand again as she turned to leave. The pain shot through me as I realized I was being locked into the small room. The grinding sound of metal against metal sounded like sturdy locks falling into place.

El was okay. I said it like a mantra. *El was okay.*

The room smelled like antiseptic.

El is okay, Sherlock repeated.

Why would the nurse say such a thing? She must have a hinge loose, herself. Or maybe she had too many patients today. I'd heard all sorts of noises behind the closed doors we'd passed. Or she might have been working a double shift if another nurse was sick.

I would've been mad if I wasn't so relieved that El was ok. I could suffer through a few more hours here. All I had to do was hold on.

I don't like these small rooms, Sherlock whispered.

I realized I didn't know much about him or his life.

My life wasn't as exciting as you might think. The cases were very stimulating, but how often is a criminal imaginative enough to interest someone like myself? How many cases involve amazing jewels or international conspiracies? I was very bored when I didn't have a decent case. Watson kept me on course. He was an amazing man. A good friend is worth everything.

I totally agreed with him.

My hand still throbbed. If Sherlock hadn't been talking, I couldn't bear it. Maybe if I walked and tried to keep my hand still as I moved? The motion made my hand throb more until my pacing matched its rhythm. Sherlock suggested that I match my breathing to the throb too.

You should try wearing disguises. I used much of my free time training myself to take on different roles. I found that very useful in my cases. Wigs and eyeglasses were always helpful. You could try adding service uniforms.

I'd like that when things got back to normal. Normal was going to be something entirely different now that Sherlock was around.

I could become a plumber with a hat pulled down over my face, or a librarian with a long skirt and a wig pulled back into a bun. It could be fun.

Finally, maybe not even an hour later or maybe more, the door to my cell opened, and Kirkland was standing there with a dark bruise on his chin.

My face felt hot. "I'm so sorry," I said and meant it.

Everything would be okay now that he'd come for me, wouldn't it?

Chapter 26

My nurse brought my clothes. She tossed them on the bed, including my shoes, after the detective left the room. I managed to move aside to protect my fingers. The sooner I was out of this place the better I thought as I dressed. I hoped that whatever was bugging my nurse would go away after she had a good night's sleep.

Kirkland was waiting for me outside.

"Thank you," I said. Any other words would have been superfluous.

His eyes softened. "I would like to keep you out of harm's way." He hesitated, waiting for my reaction.

Stunned as I was by my experience in the hospital, now I was speechless. I wasn't used to being rescued by a man, and my senses were still numbed by the medication they'd given me earlier. Thank goodness he'd come before the nurse had a chance to dose me again. Did he say something romantic?

Kirkland wrapped his strong arms around me.

I hadn't felt such peace since Harry died.

Life without Harry had been horrible. I'd been too embarrassed to tell anyone except El that when I'd kissed Harry's cold cheek that morning, I'd held his stiff form for a very long time even though I'd known he was gone. I don't think I would have let go if my cell phone hadn't been ringing incessantly. When I finally answered it, I stopped crying only long enough to gulp air. The call was from work. My manager had called Aunt Pet and all the necessary actions were set in motion.

I'd been horrified at my grotesque behavior. Now that all seemed liked it had happened to a different person.

Kirkland ended the embrace and held me at arm's length. "Are you okay?"

The polite thing would have been to say yes. As usual, I wasn't in that mode.

I was okay physically, except for the bruises around my wrists where I'd been bound to the bed—those and the embarrassing broken fingers on my right hand.

Strangely, however, I felt lighter. Less burdened. I brightened up immediately.

"I'll take that to mean yes."

I already missed those strong hands that smelled of tobacco, one of the stronger brands. What would Harry think if he could see me in the arms of another man and liking it no less? I waited for Sherlock to talk about how it didn't matter what Harry would say or at least to chide me for not getting back to the case. He was silent.

My nurse arrived. "You have to leave the hospital in a wheel chair. That's the rules."

After locking the wheels, she helped me sit down. We moved silently through the halls to the elevator. Kirkland was beside me with his hand resting on the shoulder of my good arm.

When we reached the outside doors in the lobby, I stood before she locked the wheels, anxious to walk through the glass doors that slid to either side and make good my escape. But the doors reminded me of the ones at the at the restaurant where El had been shot.

No one is going to shoot at us here.

When I glanced up, Kirkland smiled and pointed outside.

"I drove your car to the hospital. Thought you might drop me off on your way to Eccles Hospital to see El. She's asking for you." He held out my coat and helped me put my left arm through the sleeve.

"Thank you," I said again, "for everything you've done."

When I looked back, my nurse was still gripping the handles of the wheelchair tightly. Her face contorted, eyebrows lowered, and her chin pulled up to create a fierce frown. I wondered what had happened to make the nurse act like this.

"Thank you," I said to her. "I hope I wasn't too much trouble." Heaven knows what I might have done before I calmed down. I'd never physically assaulted anyone. That impulse must have been part of Sherlock's personality. Even if it didn't make sense, we were still two completely different people.

Kirkland fingered his chin.

Once we were outside with the doors safely closed behind us, I turned my attention to him. "I am very sorry." His bruised chin was turning purple. "Your chin is hard." Hard enough to break my fingers.

He smiled sheepishly. "You're a lot stronger than I would have guessed. Do you remember tackling me?"

"I can't imagine why I thought that was a good idea. That and—well—hitting you."

"I don't understand all of what happened. The one thing that I do know for sure is that you are not crazy." Then the detective laughed. The sound was huge as it boomed from his chest.

"It's a joke between El and me, the Sherlock thing."

"I thought as much. Now we have to solve the case."

The plural 'we' didn't escape me.

Very interesting, very interesting, indeed.

So, he was still here.

The sequence of events led me to believe I should withdraw until a more appropriate time.

I hadn't thought about Sherlock being around while Kirkland was embracing me. It must be very difficult for him to be trapped in me, especially since I was a woman.

I find it very interesting most of the time.

Do you really withdraw or do you hang around watching and listening to me? I suspected the latter.

Definitely not, my inner sleuth said.

I snorted. Sherlock had to have been conscious to know when to make an appearance.

"El," I turned back to Kirkland.

"Drop me off first? I need to find out if they located Mr. Randall," Kirkland responded

"Why are you looking for him?" He couldn't possibly think that Mr. Randall killed his wife or Marcus. If he found out who had killed his wife, I didn't know how he would react.

No answer.

An expletive-deletive exploded in my head. I made myself act more civil than I felt. I tried to focus on how he'd rescued me from the ward, how he'd hugged me tight, and seemed concerned about me. How he had said we. Yet he still wouldn't answer my questions.

"Drive where you want to go, and I'll take over from there."

Now that we know the facts, we don't need him. Soon, we will know the identity of the culprit.

Chapter 27

We sorted out what we knew as we drove to Eccles Hospital. Sherlock's sharp mind helped me clear away the debris in my own consciousness and focus.

There were two guns and two possible shooters.

I agree. The rifleman might not have shot the doctor or Marcus.

Kirkland might've been trying to tell us something earlier when he was talking about Louise. She wasn't here when her mother was killed.

If Louise is a sharpshooter, she wouldn't have missed. And if she shot at Miss El, I believe your friend would be dead. He'd said they were looking for Mr. Randall.

We know so little about her, about most of these people. Why would he have shot at us?

We've missed something. But all will become clear.

Sherlock was right. If we eliminated all the people without a motive or opportunity, there would be only one person left.

I think we agree that Mr. Randall loved his wife. You and El had no reason to hurt her. He must have been shooting at Jessica.

He did tell us about the patient that kept following them. If Mr. Randall had shot at them, he might have thought that we believed he lied to us.

The hospital seemed so far away. Each block made me more and more nervous until the tall building was in sight. By the time I pushed my way through the revolving doors, the sun had set. I ran through the lobby as fast as I could.

When the elevator doors opened, I wondered if I might not like small places either. But I took a deep breath and went inside.

The hospital was less than half-lit when I reached the third floor. I was sure that I'd reached a critical stage of solving Dr. Randall's and Marcus' murders.

The building was eerily quiet. The hospital itself was located in a relatively quiet area. But I expected nurses or doctors to be finishing their rounds. I glanced at my watch. It was a few minutes after seven. I must have dozed off before the Detective had found me at the other hospital.

A railing to my left overlooked the lobby below, where the clicking of heels on a hard floor approached, only to be lost as they exited the main door. Only four people had been blackmailed: Marcus, Rudy, Williamson, and Welker. What if the killer was not one of the people blackmailed?

Turning the corner to my right, a long dark corridor stretched before me. I walked softly. The left-hand wall extended for at least the length of eight rooms and the nurse's desk on the right was illuminated in the center of the floor.

I was prepared to talk the nurse into letting me sit with El even though visiting hours were long over. But she opened a file drawer and looked away from me, so there was no need.

I kept walking.

We have identified four possible motives: anger at being blackmailed which would include Williamson, Marcus, Rudy, and Dr. Welker, family problems for Mr. Randall and Louise, a desire to take over the blackmailing scheme which might include Dr. Welker or others who worked in the building and found out about her side business, or possibly a patient who had followed Dr. Randall from city to city.

Up ahead, I saw a police officer taking a nap in the darkened hallway. Having a guard posted didn't do El any good if he fell asleep on the job. Kirkland wouldn't be happy either.

I could see all of the corridor now. There was a metal door with a small glass window that probably led to stairs which I should take more often. Everything looked gray here as it did all up and down the corridor, except the walls were slightly lighter, and the carpet underfoot was a bit darker.

For the first time since I left my car, I wondered if it was a good idea coming at night to stay with El. I might only succeed in waking her up. I gently knocked on the door to her hospital room. There was no response. A blue light lit up beside one of the rooms. I heard a quiet rustling before the nurse appeared down the hall.

Assuming that the first murders had something to do with the victims of the blackmail scheme, we could eliminate Mr. Randall and his daughter. Dr. Welker was upset, but he seemed like a decent enough guy when he didn't slip into that bad mood of his. The chances of that happening with both Dr. Randall and Marcus seemed slim.

Rudy had seemed genuinely afraid when he went over to his mother's house after Marcus was killed. The same seemed to be true for Williamson too.

I asked Sherlock if he remembered what Welker had said as my mind continued to sort out the facts of the case. *That the murderer would be one of her patients. Mr. Randall could probably tell us more about why they moved so often.* The phone numbers on the mugs on Dr. Randall's desk had been for Philadelphia. I'd called there often enough when I was conferring with the Department of Human Services Regional Office to recognize the area code. The Dallas snow globe might have been a misdirection. The mugs were the important clue. But the Detective hadn't thought about who might have used the coffee cups.

All the pieces of the puzzle fit. Mr. Randall would be able to confirm the identity of the difficult patient.

I knocked again even though I didn't expect El to answer. She'd probably been given something for her pain. According to Kirkland, the bullet they removed from her shoulder had not only bore a hole into my friend—a larger one than expected—but it had also damaged the structure of her shoulder. The doctors had repaired it after removing the bullet, but it would take time to heal.

The door creaked. Even in the darkness, I could tell it was Jessica Clayborn leaning over El's bed. I'd figured out that she had a motive if she knew about the blackmail scheme, and she had the best opportunity (besides El and myself) to commit the crime. But I didn't expect to find her here.

"What are you doing?" I asked. I had figured out that Mr. Randall was the second shooter. He'd been shooting at the one person he was sure would try to continue to blackmail his wife's patients.

She backed toward the window as El opened her eyes. "I wanted to see Ms. El, see if she was seriously injured."

"She'll be fine."

What is she holding in her hand? Sherlock asked.

El groaned.

"What are you doing?" I demanded and stepped closer.

Only El's bed separated us. One of those tables that can reach across the bed like a bent arm was in front of me, turned to the side. The call button on its thick cord was dangling down to the floor next to the bed. I was about to pick it up when Sherlock interrupted me.

Do not take your eyes off of her.

As I straightened, I realized that Jessica had moved down to the end of the bed.

If El would just wake up enough to call the nurse.

"Kirkland asked me where Randall was—that weird guy and his stuck-up daughter. I made sure they would have a lot to explain. Cops said they haven't found Mr. Randall yet when I called the station," Jessica said.

"And you wanted to make sure he didn't have an alibi for El's murder."

She laughed. "You aren't as dense as you look. I think that our detective suspected me, but he'll assume Randall was trying to shoot you guys since he hit El." Jessica raised her gloved hand holding a gun. You know too much. You should have minded your own business.

"Let me guess, that's a gun registered under one of their names."

"Dr. Randall didn't know that I'd seen it in her desk. I was wondering how long it would take for you to figure out that I could have tampered with your memory. I could have disappeared after Dr. Randall was gone."

"Then why didn't you?" I asked without realizing I'd spoken. Sherlock had taken control so swiftly that I didn't have time to protest. We were now standing across from her, as close as the weapon between us allowed.

"I don't know," Jessica said, looking down.

Anger flooded Sherlock's consciousness. He grabbed the gun with my uninjured left hand, apparently as coordinated with his left hand as his right. We wrenched it away from Jessica, and he slid our finger onto the trigger. Anger filled me just as it had when El had been shot. This time, I knew it was Sherlock's anger, not mine. Just as he'd taken advantage of Jessica's moment of weakness, I took advantage of his and took over.

"Come around the bed," I barked at Jessica. While Sherlock wanted to satisfy his own sense of justice and kill this warped creature, I merely wanted to see her locked up. I'd never thought he was so blood thirsty.

As she stood before me, I felt a slight movement behind me. "I hope that's you Kirkland."

"It is," he said.

I lowered the gun.

"Shoot me," Jessica cried. She crumpled to the floor.

Kirkland took the gun from my hand.

El's new hospital room looked almost cozy in the middle of the night. The light above the bed cast a warm glow over the fresh linens like a street lamp on a snowy corner.

After the cops took Jessica away, El's surgeon showed up to make sure she was okay, and she fell asleep once more after he left. She didn't look like she'd been in surgery, except that she was so still. She hadn't moved even when they checked her vitals. I picked up her hand after the nurse left.

It was all my fault.

I was the one who took you back to Dr. Randall's office, Sherlock whispered. *And miss El had wanted to investigate too.*

If she hadn't thought I was so helpless, she could have told me that Marcus was being blackmailed. El didn't have a choice. Dr. Randall could have figured out her involvement.

I have wondered if Dr. Randall insisted that El come in the room because she knew she was trying to gather evidence.

And all Dr. Randall had to do was hypnotize El too.

El opened her eyes.

"Do you remember what happened?" I asked.

Maybe I shouldn't have said anything so soon. People probably asked their ailing relatives and friends how they felt which sounded stupid to me. She'd been shot. She had to feel like crap.

"Water?" she groaned.

I held out a glass of water that had been by her bed. El tried to reach up to hold it, but the tube sticking out of her arm got stuck on her gown. She grimaced before taking a long sip.

"That's better. Wow, it's dark outside."

"You had to stay in recovery for a while after the operation." I glanced at my watch. "It's about two in the morning."

"What are you doing here?"

"Thought you might like to see a familiar grumpy face when you woke up."

El giggled, then closed her eyes. "You should go home."

"I think I'll wait.

El didn't say anything more. I sat in silence as she slept.

Day 14
Chapter 28

El was wide awake the next day, already getting back to her old self.

"It's not fair. I don't remember what happened." She didn't look so bad, even though she winced when she moved too much.

"For some reason, Jessica was leaning over your bed when I came in the room." I moved my chair closer to her bedside.

Kirkland was leaning against the wall, arms crossed. "I knew something was up when I couldn't raise Officer Wilson on his radio. He had a bad knock on the head, but he'll be fine."

"I was afraid he was dead when I saw Jessica."

"You knew it was Jessica? Why didn't you tell me in the car?" he asked.

I opened my mouth, but El gave me a look that I knew meant she wanted me to stop talking so the detective would finish. I glared at her before responding to Kirkland.

"I suspected, but I only knew for sure after arriving at the hospital. There was only one person who had motive *and* opportunity. She always had the best opportunity to kill Dr. Randall. I didn't even consider her until I guessed that she'd worked with the doctor in Philadelphia."

"I thought they moved to Bethesda from Dallas." El was perking up.

"That's what Jessica told us. We never heard that information from anyone else," I said.

"There was a snow globe on Dr. Randall's desk from Dallas. The one from Philadelphia was up on top of the file cabinets with the others as if she'd had it for a while. The phone number on the cups on her desk had a Philadelphia area code," Kirkland said and moved to the other side of the bed.

The idea that the Randalls had moved to Bethesda from Philadelphia was so obvious, I should have thought of it sooner.

"She would naturally have had the most recent purchase on her desk," El said.

"I missed the phone numbers at first," Kirkland added. "I did have one of my juniors check with the medical societies who told us that she'd been licensed in Pennsylvania last."

"Even if she knew her from before, it doesn't give much of a motive." El was struggling to sit up. Both of us rushed to help her.

Kirkland grinned at me across the bed.

Must he smile like that when I am here?

"Dr. Welker was right all along," I said. "He said it would mostly be one of her patients. And Randall did say patients used to call all the time. Remember him talking about his wife being a victim too?"

258

"Of course! Jessica was one of her patients," El exclaimed.

"She must have followed the Randalls to Maryland."

"And she must have found out that Dr. Randall was blackmailing others, or maybe the scheme was Jessica's idea," Kirkland said and pulled up a chair on the other side of El's bed. "I'll have to ask her."

I'd thought it was lucky that they had put El in a private room until Kirkland told me that it was standard procedure. Besides no one would want to be in a room with someone who had almost been murdered.

"She blackmailed Dr. Randall into giving her a job," El finished his thought.

I didn't have much sympathy for Dr. Randall. I didn't think we would ever know how many people she'd blackmailed.

"The keys made me suspect Jessica from the beginning," Kirkland said. "I thought she might have removed some files before we were called to the scene. After she let slip that Rudy Tessmeyer was there, and we couldn't find his file, we knew the keys to the cabinets were important. But there was no way to prove that the ones Jessica had didn't belong to her."

El's eyes went wide. "Mr. Randall was trying to kill Jessica."

"I suppose he was afraid it would make him look like he was part of the blackmailing scheme and wanted her to stop. We know now that Jessica had demanded more money from at least Rudy Tessmeyer, acting as if she was doing it for Dr. Randall. That's what started everything." Kirkland's chair creaked; it was well worn.

Sherlock took over much to my surprise. "Dr. Randall must have known how volatile Jessica was before she confronted her. She must have been very angry to forget."

I was sure that El knew it was Sherlock speaking.

"Dr. Randall promised her husband she would stop," she added.

"Did she?" Kirkland asked. "That will count in his favor."

Randall would be serving time for attempted murder even if they didn't charge him with blackmail. What the other states where Dr. Randall had practiced would do was anybody's guess. Blackmail victims wouldn't be anxious to come forward.

"Where did the gun come into all of this?" El asked.

"I wish we could say that we've traced the gun back to Ms. Clayborn. We can't."

If I had been Dr. Randall, it would have been my gun. And, as Dr. Randall's employee, Jessica had more than enough opportunity to discover if Dr. Randall kept it in her desk.

"It was Dr. Randall's gun."

"Mr. Randall confessed that his wife had a gun she'd bought on the street in Philadelphia since Jessica had followed

them from Dallas. Dr. Randall was afraid of her. Randall tried to convince her not to keep the gun at work, but she told him it was okay if it was locked inside the desk." Then Kirkland patted El's arm. "I hope you're feeling better soon. I have to get back to the office. I have a lot of paperwork to do."

Bureaucracy had been the bane of my existence at one time too.

"Don't forget to check Jessica's phone. If she hasn't changed the ringtone, I bet it's a Bach fugue."

Kirkland cleared his throat. "I'll check."

El looked at me curiously. "What on earth? You wouldn't know a Bach fugue from a country western ballad. Oh," she said and widened her eyes. I imagined she was thinking that my resident sleuth would.

Getting used to Sherlock was going to take some work. But it would be much easier now that my best friend had accepted him. I breathed deeply.

Day Fourteen had been a good, non-smoking day.

THE END

CPSIA information can be obtained
at www.ICGtesting.com
Printed in the USA
BVHW031349220622
640417BV00021B/221